THE ROYAL HOUSE OF NIROLI

Always passionate, always proud.

**The richest royal family in the world—
a family united by blood and passion,
torn apart by deceit and desire.**

THE HISTORY OF NIROLI

Niroli has a colorful and fascinating history filled with ancient rivalries, rebels and kings. It is a story of kingdoms, castles and untold riches. The Fierezza family has ruled since the Middle Ages, and founded its fortune on ancient trading routes, thanks to its beautiful position to the south of Sicily.

Over centuries, Niroli prospered as an important port on major spice, wine and perfume-trading routes. After a battle as recent as 1972, they lost control of the neighboring island Mont Avellana, which became a republic. The monarchy of Niroli has been handed down through the Fierezza line. There is still a lot of resentment and rivalry between the islands. In addition to this, a group of bandits known as the Viallis, who are ex-Barbary corsairs, formed a resistance against the monarchy. The height of their rebellious activity was in the 1970s, and a few remaining Viallis still live in the foothills of the Niroli mountain range.

The Official Fierezza Family Tree

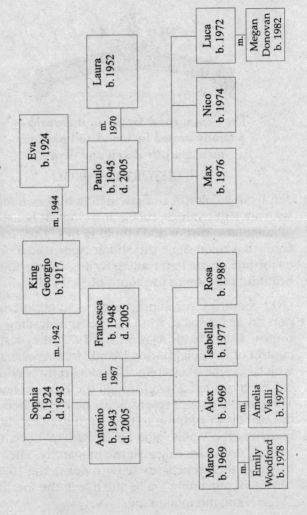

Natasha Oakley

THE TYCOON'S
PRINCESS BRIDE

THE ROYAL HOUSE OF NIROLI

Always passionate, always proud.

HARLEQUIN®

TORONTO • NEW YORK • LONDON
AMSTERDAM • PARIS • SYDNEY • HAMBURG
STOCKHOLM • ATHENS • TOKYO • MILAN • MADRID
PRAGUE • WARSAW • BUDAPEST • AUCKLAND

To Trish, Ally and Nic

ISBN-13: 978-0-373-38954-4
ISBN-10:   0-373-38954-X

THE TYCOON'S PRINCESS BRIDE

First North American Publication 2007.

Copyright © 2007 by Harlequin Books S.A.

Special thanks and acknowledgment are given to Natasha Oakley for her contribution to THE ROYAL HOUSE OF NIROLI series.

www.eHarlequin.com

Printed in U.S.A.

The Rules

Rule 1: The ruler must be a moral leader. Any act that brings the Royal House into disrepute will rule a contender out of the succession to the throne.

Rule 2: No member of the Royal House may be joined in marriage without consent of the ruler. Any such union concluded results in exclusion and deprivation of honors and privileges.

Rule 3: No marriage is permitted if the interests of Niroli become compromised through the union.

Rule 4: It is not permitted for the ruler of Niroli to marry a person who has previously been divorced.

Rule 5: Marriage between members of the Royal House who are blood relations is forbidden.

Rule 6: The ruler directs the education of all members of the Royal House, even when the general care of the children belongs to their parents.

Rule 7: Without the approval or consent of the ruler, no member of the Royal House can make debts over the possibility of payment.

Rule 8: No member of the Royal House can accept an inheritance or any donation without the consent and approval of the ruler.

Rule 9: The ruler of Niroli must dedicate their life to the Kingdom. Therefore they are not permitted to have a profession.

Rule 10: Members of the Royal House must reside in Niroli or in a country approved by the ruler. However, the ruler *must* reside in Niroli.

THE ROYAL HOUSE OF NIROLI
Always passionate, always proud.

Harlequin Presents is delighted to bring you a new series, THE ROYAL HOUSE OF NIROLI, in which you can follow the epic search for the true Nirolian king. Eight heirs, eight romances, eight fantastic stories!

The Future King's Pregnant Mistress
by Penny Jordan

Surgeon Prince, Ordinary Wife
by Melanie Milburne

Bought by the Billionaire Prince
by Carol Marinelli

The Tycoon's Princess Bride
by Natasha Oakley

Coming next:

Expecting His Royal Baby
by Susan Stephens

One by one, the heirs to the throne of Niroli are ruling themselves out. The king's health continues to decline, and his court is in turmoil. Enter the prince with a provocative past, who's returned to claim the crown....

The Prince's Forbidden Virgin
by Robyn Donald

Bride by Royal Appointment
by Raye Morgan

A Royal Bride at the Sheikh's Command
by Penny Jordan

CHAPTER ONE

HER Royal Highness, Princess Isabella of Niroli knew from the flashing pinprick of green light in the far right-hand corner of the conference room that she was being watched.

And she didn't like it. Not one bit.

She straightened her spine in one tiny, barely perceptible movement and let absolutely no emotion appear on her face. She was used to surveillance. Telephoto lenses were aggressively focussed on her every time she stepped out of doors and even the fairly basic security system in her family's fourteenth century castle was considerably more sophisticated than the one protecting Domenic Vincini's inner sanctum.

Even so...

That blinking green light made her feel irritated. She twisted the fine platinum bangle of her wrist watch so the diamond encrusted face was uppermost and looked at the time.

How much longer was she prepared to wait for Signore Vincini to put in an appearance? Five minutes? Ten? How many before she appeared too desperate?

Maybe it was already too late to think about that? Maybe by forcing this meeting she'd already undermined her bargaining position? Shown her hand too early, as her cousin Luca would say?

But…

She *wanted* this deal. Badly. It felt personal. *Was* personal. So much effort had gone into it—and for such a long time now. Two years spent carefully courting the Vincini Group of hotels, nine months of concentrated negotiations…

And, in all those months, she'd not once met Signore Vincini, the power behind the Vincini Group and the man who will ultimately make the decision.

She'd been warned that he was a man who could not be forced…or cajoled. Rumour had it that he worked like an automaton and made his judgements without reference to anything other than the 'bottom line'. In recent years he'd stopped visiting his proposed investments or, indeed, the existing hotels he owned across the Mediterranean, yet he somehow managed to keep a finger on the pulse.

Back on Niroli that had sounded exaggerated. Surely a development the size of the one they proposed would warrant a more personal involvement…but, what if it was true?

Perhaps her 'charm offensive' was, at best, pointless and at worst…

Damn.

She didn't want to think about failure. Isabella stared unseeing across the width of the conference room. There was so much resting on her ability to bring this deal together—not least her own future on Niroli. Her hand moved to twist her watch round once more. She'd give him another five minutes and then—

'Your Royal Highness?'

Isabella turned at the sound of a hesitant voice. The quietly handsome man who'd ushered her into the room twenty minutes earlier let go of the door handle and unconsciously flexed his fingers.

'M-may I offer you something to drink, Your Highness?'

'Nothing, thank you.' She smiled, and then watched with resignation the slow blush that moved up from his neck.

Why did men react like that? She'd chosen her clothes so carefully in the hope she'd be seen as something other than an elegant coat hanger. There wasn't much else she could do, short of sticking a paper bag over her head and wearing a bin liner—which probably wouldn't help her be taken seriously either.

'S-signore Vincini wondered…if…' he cleared his throat '…I might assist you? R-rather than keep you waiting any longer.'

Her eyes flicked up to the pulsing green light. Was Domenic Vincini watching this? Somehow she felt certain he was—an all-seeing omnipotent being. 'I'll wait.'

'I've been asked to say that Signore Vincini is delayed indefinitely. He sends his apologies and—'

'Then I'll wait *indefinitely*,' she said, cutting him off, her voice uncharacteristically crisp.

Isabella watched the nervous bob of his Adam's apple and allowed herself to feel a moment's sympathy, but not so much that she'd do as he wanted. She couldn't.

Whatever Signore Vincini felt about her being here, there was no point in trying to explain the complex rivalry that existed between Niroli and Mont Avellana to this man. He wouldn't understand.

No one born away from the islands would appreciate the depth of mistrust. It had been built over centuries and was practically sewn into the fabric of daily life. And, in her opinion, it was time it stopped.

She picked up her briefcase and set it out on the table. With practised fingers she manipulated the combination lock and opened the case out. 'Perhaps I might have a glass of water after all?'

A sharp frown snapped across Domenic Vincini's face as his half-sister perched her bottom on the edge of his wide desk. 'Is there something you want?'

'I've come to talk to you.'

'I'm busy,' he said, retrieving the papers she'd dislodged.

'You're always busy.' Silvana picked up his letter opener and idly ran her fingers over the pewter point, the fact that she was messing with his things was as irritating as her being here. 'You must know you can't keep her waiting for ever. She's obviously not going anywhere until she's spoken to you, so why put off the inevitable?'

'She' being Her Royal Highness, the Princess Isabella of Niroli. His eyes flicked over to the closed-circuit television screen on his desk. 'It was her choice to come without an appointment—'

'You wouldn't have given her one if she'd asked.'

Domenic sat back in his chair and looked at his half-sister. 'Because it's unnecessary,' he agreed smoothly. 'Eduardo can tell her everything she needs to know.'

'She's waiting to talk to *you*.'

'Even a Nirolian princess must have met with disappointment before.'

What was it about Princess Isabella that made everyone think it necessary for him to immediately stop what he was doing? As if he didn't know. He rubbed a tired hand over his face. She had the kind of smile that made the paparazzi scramble and strong men falter.

'Can't you sit on a chair like a normal person?' he snapped.

'No, if I did you'd ignore me. This way I know I've got your attention.' Silvana returned the letter opener to his desk and studied him for a moment. 'It would take ten minutes of your time. You do want to build on Niroli, don't you?'

'Mildly.'

She let out her breath in one go. 'You're being offered nine thousand two hundred acres with forty-two miles of water-front. This isn't a take-it-or-leave-it kind of offer, it's a fantastic opportunity.'

'It's an option—'

'It's more than that and you know it. *Damn it,* this is what you said you wanted. Years ago. This was the grand plan.'

Something to rival Sardinia's Costa Smeralda... He remembered.

'Actually, it's better. It's on *Niroli.* Twelve years ago, when we first started talking about a luxury purpose-built resort, no one thought that a remote possibility. It doesn't get more perfect than this,' his half-sister continued, her expressive hands moving as quickly as she spoke. 'Luca Fierezza's casinos already bring in the kind of clientele we need. As does the annual opera season and the very fact Niroli still has a monarchy brings a certain charm. This is everything you and Jolanda talked about doing.'

Together. They'd talked about doing it together. And on Mont Avellana. 'I'm considering it—'

'What you're doing is letting it slip through your fingers— and I don't understand why. If we don't take up the opportunity soon, then Princess Isabella will look elsewhere.'

'That's her prerogative.'

Silvana let out an exasperated scream. 'This deal is worth billions—'

'This deal will *cost* billions,' Domenic slid in quietly.

'Which you knew when you began negotiations.'

His eyes narrowed. *True.* He'd known that, but this was *Niroli.* The arguments for and against buying the land were so personal, and so interwoven, he couldn't tell which side they fell.

'So what's changed? It's not as though you're miraculously prepared to consider developing the land we have on Mont Avellana—'

With an abrupt movement Domenic sat forward. Just the mention of his birth-island caused images to flash through his mind with fierce rapidity. It hurt. Still. He picked up his fountain pen and twisted it between long, lean fingers.

Silvana bit her lip. 'I'm sorry.'

'It's nothing.' Domenic's voice sounded rough even to his own ears. *Nothing?* How could he say that? Traumatic memories crowded round, fresh and clear. He could see the fire licking through the roof. Hear the shouting. Even taste the bitter, acrid smoke in the back of his throat.

And he could smell the burning—indescribable, but unforgettable…

In the air, on his clothes, in his hair.

He swallowed painfully. After four years there should be a way of managing his experience. He ought to have found a way of keeping control and…

'I shouldn't have said that. I'm sorry. I didn't think.'

Focus on the practical. Time had taught him to concentrate on the matter-of-fact rather than his emotions. And the fact was Mont Avellana wouldn't seduce Europe's rich and famous away from Sardinia, Sicily and a fast-developing Niroli. It had the white sandy beaches, but little else when compared to its nearest neighbour.

Domenic set his pen down on the table with meticulous care. 'Are you angry I've not developed the palazzo?'

'Of course not,' Silvana said a little too quickly. She climbed off the desk and walked over to the water cooler. 'It has to be your decision. Whatever you feel is right…'

He watched as she pressed the button to fill a cup with ice-cold water. *His* decision to make. So why did he feel as though the empty palazzo was a quiet rebuke?

'Do you want any?' she asked with a look over her shoulder.

Domenic shook his head and spoke quietly. 'Mont Avellana lacks the infrastructure of—'

'I know. Nothing's in place.' Silvana walked back and pressed a light kiss on the top of his head.

But…? He waited for the 'but'. However sorry she might be, he knew his half-sister too well to think that the conversation was over.

'And I agree. Totally.' She smoothed a hand across his shoulder. 'Mont Avellana probably isn't right for us.'

Still he waited. The rest of the world tiptoed round him, fearful of saying anything that might remind him how much he'd lost. But Silvana had no such sensitivity. She just ploughed in and told him what she thought—even though she'd been standing beside him when his life had fallen apart.

Perhaps because she'd been standing there…?

'Jolanda wouldn't blame you for reacting to market circumstances, you must know that. So why haven't you signed? What's going on, Dom? This could all have been settled weeks and weeks ago.'

Domenic twisted his pen and watched the light play on the sleek metal. The 'why' was complicated. If he'd been the kind of man who believed his problems could be solved by therapy, no doubt his analyst would have had a field day on the 'why' of it.

'And why keep Princess Isabella sitting in the conference room for twenty-five minutes?'

'Eventually she'll speak to Eduardo,' he said with assumed nonchalance.

'And if she doesn't?'

Domenic shrugged. 'I dislike having my hand forced.'

Silvana sat herself in the chair on the other side of his desk. 'That's not what's happening. She's en route to Niroli and stopped off as a courtesy to—'

'That's what she told you?' he asked.

'She hasn't had to. Everyone knows she's been at the wedding in Belstenstein as King Giorgio's representative. She wore a Mariabella Ricci dress in the palest pink. Absolutely fabulous.'

Domenic stood up and walked slowly over to the large picture window with its view of the painfully modern rooftop garden. *Jolanda would have hated the angular lines.* He should never have allowed it. He looked over his shoulder. 'Perhaps a reasonable percentage might also know Rome isn't *en route* to Niroli from Belstenstein.'

'She might have other business in Rome.'

'Unlikely.' Domenic smiled grimly. Now, if there'd been a film première in Rome this weekend, a fashion show…

'You're deliberately missing the point.'

'No, you are.' He turned. 'If I decide to build on Niroli it'll be because I believe it'll be profitable. No other reason. If I decide not to, it's because I believe it won't be. But, before I commit myself to a decision either way, I want to know why Luca Fierezza has decided to concentrate on projects away from the island.'

Silvana's mouth dropped open. 'How the...*hell* do you know he's going to do that?'

'I make it my business to know. It's why I'm very good at what I do. And if he's moved his attention elsewhere there'll be a good reason for it—and I'm not about to pour billions into a development on Niroli without knowing why.' Domenic ran a finger around the neckline of his black T-shirt as the fabric irritated his neck.

'You could ask Princess Isabella.'

His right eyebrow jerked up. 'You think she'd tell me? The very fact *Princess* Isabella has made the time to come here is suspicious,' he said, sitting back down.

'Why do you say "Princess" like that?'

Domenic looked at the television monitor and at the beautiful woman sitting at the far end of the conference table. She offended him on pretty much every level, but he hadn't realised his voice reflected his private feelings so clearly.

'It can't be because she's Nirolian royalty,' Silvana spoke into his thoughts. 'You've done business with Prince Luca perfectly happily.'

'He has an excellent track record in business,' Domenic countered. 'Princess Isabella, on the other hand, does not. She owns one small and moderately successful hotel—'

'It's beautiful!'

'And her cousin, Nico Fierezza, is responsible for that. Out of the entire Fierezza family she's the only one who floats about Europe with an entourage in tow. And, frankly, I object to doing business with someone whose involvement rests on an accident of birth and her ability to fill a designer dress to perfection.'

'That's very unfair,' Silvana said quietly. 'Eduardo says he's been impressed by her commitment to this project. And he says Princess Isabella's been an active participant from the very beginning.'

'Her *name* might appear in the paperwork, but I seriously doubt she's had more to do with it than crossing her ankles at the occasional meeting.'

'Domenic—'

'If she'd walked in here quietly, without drawing attention to herself, I'd have had more respect for her. As it is…'

Silvana shook her head. 'I don't see how she could do that. She's as much a brand as the Vincini Group.'

'A brand?'

'You know what I mean. She's photographed all the time, everywhere she goes, everything she does,' Silvana said, standing up and smoothing the creases out of her linen skirt. She met his eyes, daring him to contradict her. 'And it's not because she's the granddaughter of a king that there's an entourage waiting down in the reception hall and a bodyguard outside the conference room…'

His eyes followed her as she walked towards the door, and he wondered why his staunchly republican half-sister had suddenly become such a vocal defender of Princess Isabella.

'It's because she's got paparazzi crawling out from behind skirting boards to get a shot of her. People love her. If she wears a dress by a certain designer that designer is made.'

He knew that. Everyone knew that. It was difficult to pass any newsstand without seeing her *face* on something.

'Even without Luca's casinos, Dom, Niroli has the potential to be a very glamorous resort simply because she's prepared to lend her face to it. You ought to think about that for a minute.'

Domenic rubbed his forefinger against the spike of pain in his temple.

'And I think you're wrong to leave her sitting there. It's a mistake,' Silvana said from the doorway.

Domenic let his hand fall. 'If you feel that strongly about it, why don't you speak to her?'

She stopped. 'Me?'

'On my behalf. Why not?' He looked across at her.

'Because I'm responsible for the interior design of our hotels. I've never had anything to do with acquisitions and I wouldn't know what to ask.'

'Find out why she's here. You're good at drawing people out.'

'Domenic—'

'And you're family,' he cut in firmly.

Silvana moved a small way back into the room. 'I can't—'

'Find out why Luca has decided to focus on his casinos in Queensland.' Domenic stretched out his arm, feeling the usual stiffness in his elbow. 'And try and get some indication of who the old king intends to nominate as his successor.'

'Do you think that might have something to do with Luca's leaving?'

'It's a possibility.' Domenic sat back in his chair and twisted his pen between his fingers once more. 'It's also a variable and I like as few of those as possible, particularly where King Giorgio's concerned. The man's a snake.'

His half-sister nodded. 'I'll do my best, but you may still need to talk to her yourself if she's here for anything more than a simple hello,' she said, shutting the door behind her.

Domenic swivelled his chair round so he had a better view of the monitor—and of Princess Isabella.

Why was she here? Why *now?* After months of being content to leave the complex negotiations in the hands of a skilled team, why had she decided to come to Rome? Silvana might buy the idea that she had other business, but he didn't. And the longer she was prepared to sit waiting for him, the more he doubted it.

Domenic locked his fingers and rested them against his mouth thoughtfully. The timing of her visit had to be significant. Within twenty-four hours of Domenic's hearing that Luca Fierezza had left Niroli, Princess Isabella was sitting in his conference room. It spoke of some kind of 'damage limitation'.

Perhaps…

Or perhaps not.

He sat back in his chair. Truthfully all he really wanted was a sound business reason to decline the offer. Something that would allow him to hold up his hands and tell the world it simply wasn't meant to be.

Instead he was confronted by the public relations coup that was Isabella Fierezza. More entrancing than any woman he'd ever seen in a suit. What was it about the way she wore a pair of cream trousers and matching jacket that made it instantly bewitching?

She moved her hand to twist the diamond stud in her ear and his eyes helplessly followed the movement. Was he supposed to be honoured by her visit? Dazzled by her beauty?

If it was the latter, he *was* dazzled. Undeniably. She had a…luminosity about her. An inner glow that lit her features from the inside. Business aside, it made him want things, remember things that were no longer part of his reality.

Please God Silvana would be able to stave off a meeting. There was something particularly painful about the sympathy of a beautiful woman.

And Princess Isabella *would* feel pity. She had that kind of softness about her that told him it was inevitable—and he hated sympathy. He found it even more distressing than an ignorant person recoiling from him.

Domenic shifted uncomfortably in his chair and reached forward to switch the monitor off. Then he pulled his hand across his face once more, before picking up his pen.

CHAPTER TWO

ISABELLA sat back with a sense of achievement and took a moment to admire the room she was in. The hexagonal shape of the sitting room was unusual, but it was the light streaming in from the high windows that made it so stunning. It bounced off the glass bowls filled with fresh flowers and shone off the reflective surfaces of the furniture.

'Domenic will be another five minutes,' Silvana Moretti said, sitting in the armchair opposite. 'I'm so sorry.'

It didn't matter. She *was* going to meet him. That was the important thing. If, after today, everything came crashing down around her at least she'd know there was nothing else she could have done. 'I came prepared to wait.' She smiled, intending to charm. 'And it's so wonderfully cool in here I might decide to stay for ever.'

There was an almost imperceptible hesitation. 'My brother insists on an ambient temperature in all our hotels.'

For one second Isabella wondered what Silvana Moretti had decided not to say, but when she looked again she thought she must have been mistaken.

'The summer months are sweltering,' the tiny brunette continued smoothly, 'particularly in the city.'

Isabella smiled her agreement, but every sinew in her body was straining to hear Signore Vincini's approach.

'All of the bedrooms at the Villa Berlusconi are air-conditioned for that reason, but none of the public areas. Perhaps that's something I ought to address.'

'I've read about the Villa Berlusconi. I know my brother was impressed by the sensitive conservation of—'

'Nico Fierezza is a talented architect,' a masculine voice cut in. Deep, smooth and incredibly sexy. Impossible not to register that. Her stomach clenched in recognition.

Isabella pulled air into her lungs. Please, God, she had to do this well. Too much was resting on it for her to feel totally confident in her ability to pull it off.

'I've seen some of his more recent work in Milan, and it's equally impressive.'

'Nico has a…' Isabella turned to face the man she needed to impress, stopping as her breath caught at the back of her throat. *Dear God.*

Her eyes took in the scar that ran from his forehead to a point perilously close to his left eye. '…real affinity for old…' *buildings.* She'd meant to say 'buildings', but her voice didn't hold out that long.

'Domenic, this is Her Royal Highness, Princess Isabella,' Silvana said, moving towards him. She rested a hand on his arm. 'My brother, Domenic Vincini.'

Her voice sounded muffled as Isabella struggled to meld her expectations of Domenic Vincini with the reality. A second scar, raised and vivid, ran the length of his cheek and touched the puckered scarring of a severe burn.

Domenic Vincini was a burns survivor. Why had no one told her that? Did they know?

Skin that had wrinkled like paper disappeared beneath the soft fabric of his long-sleeved T-shirt. *Severe burns.* The truth of that imploded in her mind. Whatever had happened to him? When? And why?

Her role as an ambassador for numerous charities meant she'd seen and spoken with many burns survivors. Their stories were, without exception, harrowing. People who'd emerged from a living nightmare to face months of skin grafts and painful rehabilitation.

Her voice caught as sympathy flowed through her. 'Signore Vincini.' Then she forced her legs to move. 'Thank you so much for finding the time to see me.'

But she'd been too slow. She knew it by the flicker in his brown eyes. There was a slight hesitation before he reached out his hand to meet hers.

'Domenic.' His voice was crisp, his handshake firm.

Isabella kept her gaze firmly on his face, sheer willpower stopping her from looking to see whether he also had scars on his hands. 'And I'm Isabella. I was particularly anxious to talk to you personally.' His skin felt smooth beneath her fingers. Strong. Warm.

'So I've been told.'

'You need to see these photographs, Domenic,' Silvana said.

Domenic Vincini had a hard face, strong and uncompromising and, right now, it looked particularly unyielding.

'Why?' he asked, releasing her hand.

Isabella lifted her chin a fraction more, refusing to be intimidated by his monosyllabic question. 'Because the proposed citing of the resort is on the south coast—'

'I'm aware of that.' His voice sliced across hers.

'Which means it has spectacular views of Mont Avellana,' she said, as though he hadn't spoken.

His eyes flicked towards his sister and then back to her. 'And you think that might help swing my decision in your favour?'

'In favour of the project. Yes, I think it might.'

'Then I'd better see them.' Domenic turned away, angry at himself for having so little control over his emotions, angry at Silvana for putting him in this position.

If he'd thought his feelings about Niroli and about Mont Avellana were complicated, his feelings about Princess Isabella were even more so. He should have all the natural antipathy of a self-made man towards a woman who'd made a career out of her hereditary title, but nothing could have prepared him for the feel of her hand in his.

The lightest touch from her fingers had sent long-forgotten impulses coursing through his body. Hot, raw need. Painful in its intensity. In that second he'd known the agony of wanting to pull her into his arms, feel her body warm against his—and of knowing it was an impossibility.

She moved towards the sofa, seemingly oblivious to the thunderbolt that had shot through him. Once he might have been able to attract a woman like Isabella Fierezza, but no longer. He'd seen the shock in her hazel eyes when she'd looked at him. The instinctive recoil.

'Shall we sit down? Make ourselves comfortable?' Silvana asked, her eyes casting a reproachful look in his direction. He deserved it, he knew, but he felt so helpless. Like a dinghy out of control he could only react to the power of the storm raging inside him.

Isabella turned and smiled at him. Her eyes shone with gentle kindness—and it shamed him. If he hadn't seen her instinctive reaction to him he might have been able to convince himself she could see the man beneath the scarring, but he'd long since accepted that would never happen.

Women who claimed an attraction to him were, in reality, attracted to his money. And for good reason. His money was the most attractive thing about him since the fire. The tragedy had robbed him of everything.

'May I see the photographs now?' he said, without moving and his voice stripped of any warmth.

'Of course.' Isabella perched on the edge of the sofa and gracefully crossed her ankles. 'I realise your time is limited.'

She looked up suddenly and he felt the blood pump round his body. Her eyes were wide, a little questioning, as though she'd noticed the way he was looking at her.

Domenic sucked in his breath and willed his body to relax.

'Do you want an espresso, Domenic?' Silvana asked, moving round him to sit in one of the armchairs. 'I was about to send for some?'

'Please.' He dragged a hand through his hair. The very fact that Silvana had judged it necessary to stay for this meeting was an indictment of his behaviour. His half-sister walked over to a small telephone and spoke quietly.

Isabella leant forward and unzipped the inner pocket of her briefcase, pulling out a presentation file. Her fingers were long, thin, with perfectly manicured nails. *High maintenance.* That was what Jolanda would have called a woman like Isabella Fierezza.

'Why do you think I need to see photographs of Mont Avellana?' He was aware of Silvana beside him, felt her tension as though she doubted his ability to manage this situation.

That should have been criticism enough, but the charm and

ease that shone from Princess Isabella exacerbated it. In her company he felt ill-bred and boorish, but he was hanging by a thread. This was the best he could do. 'I know what the island looks like.'

His brusqueness was rewarded with a smile that had his blood pressure soaring. 'You were born there. I know.'

'And you think that has something to do with my reluctance to commit to your proposal?'

She reached up to finger the diamond drop that hung in the hollow of her throat. A tiny movement and the only thing that betrayed any sort of nervousness. Domenic wished he could bite back the question. The words were acceptable enough, but his tone had not been.

'Your reputation would suggest not,' Isabella said quietly. 'Certainly my team thinks it's an irrelevance.'

'But you disagree?'

'I think it might be a factor in it,' she said, meeting his eyes and holding his gaze.

He liked her ability to do that. And, in his experience, it was rare. The vast majority of people would have buckled beneath his acerbic tongue by now, certainly wouldn't have issued so obvious a challenge.

'I know it would affect mine if our situations were reversed.'

Silvana sat in the chair beside him. 'There's no doubt many people on Mont Avellana will feel betrayed if we build a luxury resort on Niroli.'

'And I can understand that.' Isabella let her hand fall from the diamond. 'Niroli is in my blood in the same way as, I imagine, Mont Avellana is in yours—'

'Whatever I might feel about my birthplace, Niroli has an established tourist industry which Mont Avellana lacks. Your team is right—anything else is irrelevant. Emotions have no place in business.'

Yet wasn't that *exactly* what he was doing here? Mixing his emotions in with what should be a purely business decision? Even if they were not for the reasons Princess Isabella was supposing.

The door opened and a waiter walked in carrying their coffee on a small tray. Silvana looked up and smiled her thanks. 'Domenic's quite right when he says there's very little in the way of an established tourist industry on Mont Avellana.'

'I'd heard that.'

'There've been two decades of consistent under-investment,' Silvana said as the door shut. 'Several years ago now, Domenic bought the Palazzo Tavolara with the intention of turning it into a Vincini hotel but the timing has never felt quite right.'

Palazzo Tavolara.

Isabella knew that Domenic Vincini now owned the Palazzo Tavolara. She'd thought she was resigned to that, but her reaction to hearing Silvana refer to it was completely in-stinctual.

She'd been brought up to feel resentment. Taught to believe the Palazzo Tavolara had been stolen from the Fierezza family. Tension expanded in her head. It was almost like a time bomb waiting to go off at any moment.

'Certainly we couldn't consider building a resort there,' Silvana continued, passing across an espresso. 'Funnily enough, Domenic and I were talking about that earlier this afternoon.'

Isabella scarcely heard the final sentence. She reached out for her coffee and sipped, grateful she had an action to hide behind.

Domenic Vincini might be able to leave his emotions out of his business decisions, but she couldn't. Emotion was at the heart of everything she'd ever done. She was only here at all because she loved Niroli, she felt as connected to it as if it were by umbilical cord.

And, deep down, she didn't believe he could separate his life into neat compartments either. He'd been born on Mont Avellana. He couldn't have escaped being shaped by the war that had driven their two islands apart.

Domenic leant forward to pick up his own coffee. 'Perhaps that wasn't the most sensitive comment, Silvana.'

His voice held a different tone, which cut through her thoughts. Isabella looked up to find he was watching her and she had the strangest sensation he'd known exactly what she'd been thinking. Understood what she was feeling and, more surprisingly, had empathy for it.

'I don't think my sister is aware that the Palazzo Tavolara was built by the Fierezza family,' he said dryly.

The hard glitter had disappeared from his eyes. They were kind and entirely *different* somehow.

'Oh, hell!' Silvana said, her hand coming up to cover her mouth. 'I'm so sorry. I didn't think.'

Isabella shook her head, not needing or wanting Silvana to feel awkward. 'Both sides of the conflict had land and property confiscated.' She searched out the unexpected warmth in Domenic's eyes. 'I've only seen photographs of the palazzo, of course. I was told it was badly damaged during the war?'

'It's structurally sound, but many of the original features were looted. She's wounded, but still very beautiful.'

He smiled and she found her own mouth curve in a genuine response. Domenic Vincini was a man of contradictions, it seemed. 'I'm glad. It was my grandmother's favourite home.' She hesitated. There probably would never be a more perfect opening to say what she'd come to say. 'I understand your family, too, had land confiscated?'

'Land you're now offering to sell me back. The irony of it hasn't been lost on me.' Domenic picked up his espresso. His eyes glinted above the rim of his cup. 'Is that why you're here? Because you've only just realised the connection I have with Niroli?'

She swallowed painfully, unsure of what she felt about him. She was unsure, too, how to answer that question. There was so much she could have said about why she'd come to Rome and *why* she was so anxious to stop this deal disintegrating around her.

Isabella looked up into his dark eyes. He was calmly waiting for an explanation. She'd forced a meeting on him and now couldn't think what to say.

And, yet, it was all so clear in her head. She was here to offer him a common sense solution to something she suspected was the real issue behind the delays.

But she might be wrong. All reports about the way Domenic Vincini did business suggested she was. Isabella fingered the diamond stud in her ear. It was too late to back down now. She'd made her decision when she'd arranged to come to Rome rather than fly directly home.

'No,' she said quietly, but quickly gaining confidence. 'Though I admit there was more concern over your family's connection to the resistance than the land we confiscated from your mother's family.'

She knew by his body language that she had his attention. 'The Vincini name is remembered…and—'

'Hated?'

Isabella shook her head. 'Resented. Deeply.'

His mouth twisted. 'Then why approach us? There are many consortiums who would be interested in what you're offering.'

Vaguely she heard Silvana murmur his name, but she ignored it. This was between the two of them. 'But few have the client base you do…or the reputation for excellence. I want something that will rival the Costa Smeralda. Exceed it.'

He roughly set his espresso cup down on the table and she feared she was losing him. Her heart thumped against her rib cage. 'I want Niroli to be the first choice for Europe's rich and famous.'

'I accept that what *we* are would complement Niroli, but, as you've already said, my family have owned land there before and had it snatched away. What guarantees have I got?'

'My grandfather is fully supportive of this venture.'

'Long term that's no guarantee. Times change.'

Monarchs changed. And King Giorgio was elderly. He didn't have to say that for Isabella to know what he was thinking. Nor could she give any guarantees. Six months ago she'd been certain what lay ahead for Niroli. But, now…everything was changing so quickly—and her position with it.

'That's true. But, like Mont Avellana,' Isabella began carefully, 'Niroli was damaged by the war of independence. It was costly in terms of lives and money and I don't honestly believe anyone wants to see that kind of violence again.'

Isabella saw the slight narrowing of his eyes. Whether that was good or bad she couldn't tell, but she knew he was listening intently. 'And I don't believe you think it's likely either. If you did you'd have said no months ago.'

Almost he smiled. There was the tiniest quirk of his mouth, quickly suppressed.

'But if our situations were reversed I think I'd find it difficult to contribute to Mont Avellana's success, particularly if I thought it might have an adverse effect on Niroli. We've all been pretending the old prejudices don't exist, but I think everyone in this room knows they still do.'

She stopped. For a moment there was silence. Isabella looked from brother to sister and back again, trying to gauge their reactions. 'For the past two years I've been told you would not be interested in anything other than the profit margin, but…'

'But you don't believe that?'

Isabella moistened her lips. 'I think if that were true you'd have signed by now. We're a sound investment. The only real negative I can see from your perspective is that we're Niroli.'

He sat back in his chair and touched the tips of his fingers. The eyes that watched her were thoughtful.

'Domenic was concerned that Luca—'

He stopped Silvana with a shake of his head. 'What are you proposing?'

The intensity of his gaze unnerved her, but she resolutely held out the presentation file she'd had resting on her lap. He needed to see how beautiful Mont Avellana looked from Niroli. How romantic.

Domenic leant forward and took the file from her. His fingers hesitated before he flicked open the top cover.

'That's the view that your hotels would look out on.' She knew that the image was a powerful one. Caught just as the sun was rising.

He said nothing, but he pulled a hand through his hair. Isabella didn't stop to try and analyse what Domenic was feeling, she ploughed on. 'Anyone looking out on that each morning will want to go there. Even though I've been taught to feel…' She waved her hand and searched for the word that would convey her family's anger at having to give up sovereignty of Mont Avellana.

'I understand,' Domenic said.

Isabella swallowed. 'Even though I've heard so many terrible stories about Mont Avellana I've always wanted to go there. And if I feel that, how much more will people who haven't been taught to think as I have?'

Her words pooled in the silence.

Domenic looked back down at the image, then his fingers turned the page. Photograph after photograph. Isabella knew she'd caught the magical beauty of Mont Avellana.

'I was thinking that the proximity of the new development to Mont Avellana could work to the advantage of both. Why shouldn't there be boat trips from the resort across to the cave I've read about, for example?'

'Poseidon's Grotto,' Silvana clarified, her eyes on her brother. 'How do you know about that?'

'It's in my grandmother's diary.' Isabella looked from one to the other. 'I was thinking we might build links with the best of the local restaurants, certainly develop the diving opportunities. It's the obvious thing to do because Niroli already draws a significant number of diving enthusiasts.'

Domenic looked up. 'Encourage diving among the wrecks?'

'Yes.'

In the silence that followed Isabella felt as though she could hear her heart beating. A solid thud. She watched as he flicked through the file once more and forced her hands to remain relaxed in her lap.

She'd never wanted anything quite so much, or been so entirely unsure of the ultimate outcome.

CHAPTER THREE

'SO, ARE you optimistic?'

'About Domenic Vincini?' Isabella looked up from the newborn baby in her arms as Bianca curled herself in the corner of the sofa. 'Truthfully?' She grimaced. 'I've no idea. He's a difficult man to read.'

Her friend laughed. 'So I'm told. I'm sure you managed him brilliantly. All men are putty in your hands.'

'Not this one.' She smiled. 'But it was worth a try. If he doesn't sign on the dotted line now I think I'm going to have to accept he's not going to. Niroli has nothing to offer him he doesn't already know about.'

'What will you do then?'

'Don't know. Move. Start again.' She shrugged. 'I'm sure I'll think of something. I should probably have left Niroli years ago anyway.'

'Like your sister?'

'Perhaps.' Isabella looked back down at the sleeping baby, his tiny mouth pursed in seeming concentration.

She envied Bianca this. Husband, home, baby… Was it wrong to feel so dissatisfied with her life? To want something so spectacularly 'normal'? 'Fabiano's beautiful,' she said, stroking the soft skin of his cheek.

'When he's asleep.'

Isabella placed her forefinger against his hand and marvelled at the reflex action that brought his tiny fingers round it. 'You don't mean that. He's a little miracle. Aren't you?' she said softly, stroking the fingers.

Fabiano's tiny mouth pursed tighter and then he hiccupped, his body racked with the sudden onslaught. 'Oh, darling,' Isabella murmured, moving him to rest against her shoulder. Her hand moved rhythmically against his back. 'Does that hurt you, little one?'

Bianca smiled, watching. 'You ought to be a mother. You're a natural.'

'Chance would be a fine thing. The men I meet are too interested in my money and title.' She kept her voice light, but it was an effort. Fabiano's body was warm against her chest and he smelt of baby and talcum powder. There was nothing more perfect than that clean newborn smell.

She also loved the way his legs were still tucked up underneath him, much as he would have been in the womb. He was achingly perfect. Isabella rubbed her own cheek against the softness of his head. *The chance would be a very fine thing.*

'Tell me about Domenic Vincini. What's he like?'

Like? Isabella's hand moved soothingly across Fabiano's back. She thought for a moment. Like no one she'd ever met before. Just not an easy man to sum up in a few words.

She'd expected someone powerful—and he was, but not in the mould of her brother Marco, or her grandfather. Not like that at all. He was... She frowned. He was confusing. She wasn't at all sure what she made of him.

'Is he ugly?'

'Ugly?'

Bianca shrugged. 'I thought he was badly scarred. I'm sure I heard that.'

'He is. But, not ugly.'

Not ugly at all. She frowned. But not precisely attractive either. More charismatic. Certainly confusing. She wasn't at all sure whether she'd liked him. At first she'd been certain she didn't and then almost certain she did.

He'd been brusque. And he'd been kind.

And his eyes…

Deep, deep brown. Fearsomely intelligent. He looked like a man who would have an opinion on most things. Strong.

A man who was not overly impressed by her. She smiled and kissed the top of Fabiano's head. After a weekend of being fêted and photographed that had made a change.

Domenic Vincini hadn't tried to hold her hand too long. He hadn't pawed at her—or stood too close. He hadn't been obsequious or overly complimentary. In fact, he'd not been complimentary at all.

'He's got a scar that goes from here to here.' She moved her hand down the side of her face. In fact, he'd had two scars. Deep set, but not fresh. 'They're not ugly, but they're very noticeable.' In fact, they were shocking—partly because without them he'd have been spectacularly attractive.

Isabella lifted Fabiano off her shoulder and settled him back in the crook of her arm. 'And he's got a burns scar on his neck. Keloids—is that what they call them?'

Her friend pulled a face. 'You'd be more likely to know that than me.'

'Do you know how he got them?'

'In a house fire.' Bianca pulled her legs up tight against her chest and wrapped her cotton skirt around her ankles. 'I think. At least that's what everyone says. His wife and baby died in it.'

Died? Had Bianca really said that? Isabella looked up from Fabiano.

'Several years ago now.' Her friend twisted her hair back into a high topknot. 'I don't think I ever heard the details because it was a good couple of years before my time. Stefano would know more than me since his parents now live a few kilometres from where it happened. I could ask him about it if you like?'

Isabella shook her head. 'No one had warned me. It came as a bit of a shock.'

'I suppose it's the kind of thing people tend not to talk about because they don't know what to say.'

'Even so…' Surely someone would have thought to have mentioned something so significant. Luca? Surely he knew?

Bianca smiled, attuned to her thoughts. 'You need more women on your team if you want that kind of information. Perhaps I should have said something, but it's not exactly relevant when it comes to a business deal and I didn't think.' Fabiano stirred and let out a piercing scream. 'There he goes,' she said, reaching for her son. 'He's hungry again. Not surprising really. He's slept for almost four hours.'

Isabella handed Fabiano across and watched with a pang as Bianca concentrated on latching her baby onto her left breast. Her friend's face momentarily contorted and then she looked up with a smile. 'He's on.'

'Good.' She looked away, mainly because it was painful to watch something so intimate. It tightened the knot of dissatisfaction within her just that little bit more.

'Do you have to fly back to Niroli tomorrow? It seems such a long time since I saw you.'

Isabella smiled. 'You'd soon get tired of having paparazzi camped outside your door.'

'I wouldn't. I—'

The door opened and a maid came forward with a note. 'There's been a letter delivered for Her Royal Highness,' she said, nervously holding out a heavy cream envelope.

'Thank you, Caryn.' Isabella held out her hand and raised her eyebrows in Bianca's direction. 'Who'd write to me here?' She slid a finger underneath the gummed flap and pulled out a single sheet of paper. Handwritten in strong, black strokes.

'Well?'

'It's from Domenic Vincini.'

'How does he know you're here?'

'I told his sister.' Isabella frowned as she read on. There wasn't much to take in. Short, precise…and very much to the point.

'Silvana?'

Isabella looked up. 'That's right. She was at the meeting today.'

'I like her. She's his half-sister, you know.'

No, she didn't know. She frowned. Another thing she hadn't been told.

Bianca inserted a finger to detach Fabiano from her breast. She switched sides. 'What does Domenic want then?'

'Dinner.'

Bianca's eyebrows shot up. 'I told you they all become putty.'

'No, not that.' *Definitely not that.* 'Business.'

'That's great!'

Was it? Possibly. Isabella wasn't so sure. All of a sudden she felt as though a million butterflies had been loosed in her stomach.

Domenic knew the minute Princess Isabella arrived. On the monitor he saw the sudden surge of paparazzi towards her, watched the practised smile, the quiet skill of her bodyguard in detaching her.

He pulled a hand through his hair and wondered, for perhaps the hundredth time, what he was doing this for. Silvana had been in favour, but then Silvana would favour anything that would coax him back to Mont Avellana.

And who was to say she wasn't right? At some point he was going to have to face his demons. Although this time his demons would have to wait. There was nothing that couldn't be delegated.

Switching off the monitor, he stood up. Pausing only to straighten the report he was reading so that it rested at right angles to the desk, he picked up his jacket and headed out towards the lift.

Not a date. Not by any means a date—but he felt nervous, like his teenage self going to meet Jolanda. So many years ago now. Eighteen. No. Nineteen. *Nineteen years.*

Domenic unrolled the sleeves of his white shirt and shrugged himself into his dinner jacket. He had to keep at the forefront of his mind that this was business. Business was what he did best. The lifeline that had kept him breathing in and out day after day…

But it didn't feel like business when he stepped out onto the sixth-floor *terrazzo*. The combination of lemon trees, white flowers and Roman lamps that decorated it made it appear almost bridal. If there'd been time he would have asked that they removed the candles from the single dining table. It created entirely the wrong mood…

He turned at the sound of footsteps, braced to see her again. Where was the wisdom in this? But, there was no time to think about that now as his *maître d'* opened the door and ushered the princess out.

And she looked like a princess. Her rich honey-blonde hair was piled on her head, soft tendrils left to frame her face. *God, but she was beautiful.* Like a May morning. Fresh, and full of promise.

Domenic's feet seemed leaden. He knew he ought to move towards her, to welcome her…but his feet refused to move.

The warm summer breeze caught at the light silk of her dress. She looked different from this afternoon. More relaxed… Approachable and incredibly sexy. In a different life he would have wanted to kiss her. And he knew that her lips would feel warm. Totally seductive.

He stepped forward. 'Your Royal Highness.' His voice was low, but clipped.

'Isabella. Please.'

Isabella. She reached out her hand and he took hold of it. Her palms were warm and her fingers were cold. He looked up—and her eyes were like molten toffee.

Bad idea! This was a truly bad idea. At some deep, fundamental level he responded to this woman. God only knew why. Perhaps it was nothing more than recognition of her undeniable beauty? Perhaps a consequence of his celibacy?

But he knew it was more than that. It felt like a meeting of souls.

She was looking at him, her black-lashed eyes taking in the scars on his face. Seeing the slashing red ridges that would always remind him of failure. Of loss.

Domenic pulled in a breath, difficult in the still heavy air. 'Thank you for coming at such short notice.'

And then she smiled. If he thought he'd been suffering before, he knew now that was nonsense. Her smile ripped through all his defences. He ached for a woman like Isabella.

Loneliness was part and parcel of who he was now. It was part of his day-to-day existence, but it felt like a razor slicing through flesh to be on the receiving end of a smile like that.

The breeze tugged at the corkscrew curl that brushed against one of the the long silver-coloured droplets that hung at her ears. His eyes followed the length of her neck, helplessly taking in the small hollow at the base of her throat.

He would not allow his eyes to travel any further. Not to the matching necklace with the equally long droplet that nestled between her full breasts…

Oh, God.

This felt like a reawakening. For four years he'd scarcely noticed whether the people around him were male or female. He noticed competence, general efficiency…

He never registered perfume. *Never.* But he knew that from this moment Isabella Fierezza would always be associated in his mind with the scent of vanilla and musk. It hovered on her skin, enticing and beguiling.

'I was pleased I could come. I fly back to Niroli tomorrow morning.'

Domenic released her hand and stepped back. The *maître d'* moved to guide Isabella towards the table. As she walked away from him he had the most perfect view of her bare back.

His eyes followed the line of her spine until it dipped behind the light silk of her dress.

A wise man would back away now, but perversely he liked to feel the pain. It felt right that he should suffer…

'This is beautiful,' she murmured, looking out towards the *Trinità dei Monti*.

It was more than the perfect symmetry of her face; it was something that shone from inside her. Something that meant he reacted to her in a way he'd never done when seeing a photographic image of her.

'I love the feeling of being on top of the world. To watch what's going on without being seen.' She looked back and smiled, unfazed by the fact he was studying her so closely. 'I have a small private terrace at the Villa Berlusconi where I can watch the early evening *passeggiata*. Everyone dressed up and eating *gelato*.'

Domenic swallowed and took a step back. 'Privacy, I think that's called.'

And she laughed. 'You're probably right,' she said, sitting down. 'I have precious little of that. My fault, of course.'

Which was exactly what he'd thought about her. A woman that courted publicity, loved the attention she got. But nothing was ever quite as it seemed, was it? There was a wistful edge to her voice, hidden by a quick smile and a determined cheerfulness.

He took the seat opposite and nodded at the *maître d'* to offer to pour wine into her glass.

'I would prefer mineral water. Please.'

'Don't you drink?'

'Rarely.'

He understood so much more than she'd put into words.

He heard the finality in her 'rarely'. Understood that Princess Isabella was always on duty, constantly aware that a picture of a high-profile and inebriated royal would be syndicated around the world.

A simple movement of his wrist had the *maître d'* remove both their wineglasses.

'Please, don't let me stop you—'

Domenic shook his head. 'I'm no great lover of alcohol these days.' And a clear head this evening was a necessity.

She looked at him as though she had a question forming, but had thought better of asking it. He was grateful for that. What would she think if he'd told her that, particularly in the early days, anything that numbed the pain, even for a few hours, was welcome?

She looked away, out over the darkening skyline and then back. 'I do have to break my rule occasionally, though.' She smiled. 'My cousin Max is a passionate advocate of Niroli's Porto Castellante Blanco and he'd never forgive me if I refused a glass when there was an opportunity to publicise it.'

'We stock it here. If that's your preference I can—'

She smiled again, her teeth white and perfect. 'You do?'

'It's an excellent wine. Dry. Good with fish.'

Her smile became almost impish and he felt his gut tighten yet further.

'I know it's sacrilege to say it, but I've never really liked it.' Her hand brushed at the hair floating across her cheek. One single strand of warm honey-gold. 'Nor am I particularly fond of rainbow mullet, even though it is our signature dish and, I'm sure, perfectly delicious.'

Domenic gave a crack of laughter, simply because it was so unexpected.

'Or squid. Which is totally revolting.'

He smiled, feeling his body relax. Almost. He would never be able to entirely relax around Princess Isabella. No man could. 'I believe we're having Spicy Rack of Lamb with Sweet and Sour Caponatina, but, of course, if there's something else you'd prefer…?'

'That sounds perfect,' she said quickly. 'It was thoughtless of me to express any opinion before I knew what your chef had prepared for me.'

Domenic smoothed an invisible crease out of the starched white tablecloth. She had manners as charming as her face. 'The price of royalty?'

'I made a deal with the devil when I was too young to know what it would mean,' she said, pulling herself straighter in her chair. He watched the tentative smile and wondered at the vulnerability behind it. 'It's too late now to start complaining that I have no anonymity and that people go to extraordinary lengths to impress me.'

'And it would be rude to disappoint them?'

'Hurtful,' she agreed. 'And why do that if you can avoid it?'

Why? She stated it as though it were a fact. Domenic sat back in his chair. 'Do you ever want to kick over the traces?' he prompted. 'Rebel? Do something entirely for yourself?'

'Often. I thought I'd schedule it in as some kind of midlife crisis.'

She was joking, but there was a clear underlying core of truth in her words. Isabella Fierezza's life was one of duty.

And, right now, her life was chafing. The façade she presented to the world was almost perfect, but he knew more than most what it felt like to hide.

* * *

Domenic Vincini was easy to talk to. *Very easy.* She hadn't expected that, but then from the very first moment of setting eyes on him he'd defied expectation.

She'd deliberately set out to make him feel comfortable—and she was fairly sure she'd succeeded. More unexpected was that she'd been able to relax herself. She pushed a spoon into her melting chocolate cakelet and let the rich dark chocolate ooze out onto the white plate.

Luca had said that he was a trustworthy businessman. Right at the beginning when she'd had to fight with her grandfather for the possibility of approaching the Vincini Group he'd told her that. And he was right. Domenic was certainly trustworthy. She felt confident that whatever she said would go no further.

There were precious few people she could say that about. She'd learnt the hard way that the nicest of people could be corrupted. Letters, gifts, conversations. Nothing was sacred.

She closed her eyes as she tasted the rich perfection of the chocolate sauce. Dark, smooth and not cloyingly sweet. It was yet more proof, if more were needed, why she wanted the Vincini Group behind Niroli's luxury resort. Everything that happened within one of Domenic Vincini's hotels was flawless from the minute you walked through the door to the minute you left.

'Good?'

'Food fit for the gods,' she said with a smile. 'How do you find your chefs?'

His eyes glinted. 'That would be telling.'

She laughed. Then, scared though she was to hear the answer, it was time to find out why he'd decided to ask her back. Isabella snatched a quick breath and asked the question before she lost her nerve. 'What did you want us to discuss?'

Domenic rested his spoon down on the edge of his plate and rubbed a hand across his face. His fingers smoothed over the deep scars that scored down the left hand side of his face.

It was strange, but until that moment she'd almost stopped noticing them. Now her eyes searched out the puckered skin that ran down the left side of his neck, clearly visible because he chose not to, or could not, wear a tie.

Ugly?

Perhaps. But the story behind the scars was likely to be uglier still. She'd heard experts talk about the 'hidden scars', the ones that didn't show on the body but were buried deep in the psyche of burns survivors.

Quite deliberately she pulled her eyes away and concentrated on taking another mouthful of her dessert.

'The photographs you brought me were…interesting.' She looked up again. 'And I agree with you that anyone sitting out on their terrace each morning would want to visit Mont Avellana…'

'But?' she prompted when he paused.

He looked at her, and then smiled, a slow tilting of his mouth. 'It's not going to be easy for people who've habitually mistrusted each other to put that aside—even if it does mean jobs and increased prosperity.'

Isabella laid down her own spoon. 'I was thinking I could invest my own money in a handful of projects on Mont Avellana. It would be—' she broke off, searching for the right words '—a show of trust.' She wrinkled her nose. 'That's not quite right. A show of commitment.'

Another pause while he considered it. Isabella almost didn't dare breathe in case she missed his reply.

'That might help.' He picked up his mineral water. 'This is indelicate, but I have to ask. Would that be Fierezza family money? Or money from your personal funds?'

'Does it make a difference?'

'I think it does.' His eyes met hers above the rim of his glass and the expression in them was almost apologetic. 'Fierezza money promised now might not be forthcoming if Niroli should have a new king in the near future.'

Isabella reached up and pulled at her earring. She might have expected a response like this if she'd paused long enough to think about it. Marco's decision to relinquish his claim to the Niroli throne had far reaching consequences. It spread uncertainty like ink in water. 'I have a personal fortune.'

'Forgive me…' Domenic's strong hands splayed out on the white tablecloth '…but you'll need considerable funds at your disposal if you're to make any kind of impact on Mont Avellana.'

She felt the familiar prickle of irritation. Did he honestly think she didn't know that? Why was it so hard for anyone to take her seriously? 'I'm aware of that!' She met his gaze squarely. 'How many millions are you thinking I'll need?'

'I would think one and a half would be a reasonable starting point.'

'Then we don't have a problem.'

Domenic smiled and she fancied she could detect the supercilious superiority she found in so many men, particularly those in her family when he asked, 'Immediately available?'

Damn it! She wasn't an idiot. 'Certainly.'

His right eyebrow rose at that. 'Have you done any kind of feasibility study?'

'There's no point unless you're committed to Niroli.'

'Which still requires me to trust you.'

'Yes.' And that was the crux of the issue. Did he? Could he? Her heart thudded and she willed her breathing to stay steady.

'Have you ever been to Mont Avellana?' he asked after a moment.

Isabella brushed a hair off her face. 'No.'

'No,' he repeated.

'You haven't visited Niroli either.'

She watched a slow smile start at the edge of his mouth. He sat back in his chair. His dark eyes didn't leave her face. 'I'm prepared to sign on one condition.'

'Which is?'

'You need to visit Mont Avellana. Yourself.'

Isabella couldn't have been more shocked than if he'd stood up and yanked the tablecloth from beneath their plates. 'I can't do that.'

'Why?'

'It wouldn't be safe.'

'In what way?' he asked, mildly.

She thought of the stories her grandfather had recounted, the horrors of a brief but vicious war. 'No member of my family has been there since nineteen seventy-two.'

'Which is rather the point.' He sat forward again. 'Silvana says that people follow where you lead. If you visit Mont Avellana you'll immediately raise its profile.'

Isabella felt as though her stomach were about to climb into her throat.

'And if you're serious about bringing our islands closer, I can't think of a more effective way of achieving it.'

Her mouth felt dry. 'If I come you'll sign?'

'Yes. Whether you ultimately decide to invest in projects of your own on Mont Avellana or not.'

She was so close to pulling off the biggest deal in the history of Niroli. So very close. She could smell the victory. See the disbelief on the face of the sceptics who'd said it wouldn't happen.

'How long for?'

'Long enough for people to notice you're there. Shall we say two weeks?'

'I can't possibly stay that long!'

He shrugged.

'Three days. I could manage that.'

'A week.' Domenic smiled. 'And that's my final offer.'

Isabella reached up and pulled at her earring. 'Is it safe? For me, I mean?'

'As safe as it is for you anywhere I imagine.'

At that she laughed. He could have no idea what her life was like. 'I need protection everywhere I go now. Even on Niroli.'

'There's no reason you can't travel with your usual entourage.'

Go to Mont Avellana? Could she? Her grandfather would be apoplectic.

Isabella pushed back her seat and walked over to the edge of the *terrazzo*. She could hear laughter and the smoky sound of jazz carried along on the night air.

Mont Avellana.

Marco wouldn't hesitate. Luca, Alex…they'd all defied the king when his will had crossed theirs. Could *she?*

The big difference was that she was a woman. In his grandsons he tended to see defiance as strength and leadership potential. In his granddaughters it was less attractive. Perhaps even less so in her than in Rosa.

'Where would I stay? If I came?'

'There are two obvious choices—' He broke off as the *maître d'* returned to clear the table.

As soon as his footsteps disappeared, Isabella turned. Domenic hadn't moved. He was sitting, watching her, his face calm as though he knew her decision had already been made.

'Silvana is prepared to offer you the use of her home for the duration of your visit, although we would have to change the venue of my father's party. Or…' his voice was bland '…you could stay at the Palazzo Tavolara.'

She knew she must have betrayed some emotion when he added, 'Unless you would find that awkward.'

Isabella returned to the table and sat opposite him. Staying there wouldn't be 'awkward', but it would be strange. Good or bad, she couldn't possibly say. For years she'd longed to see what it looked like. 'Is it habitable?'

'Yes.' His long fingers picked up a grape from his plate. 'And its advantage over Silvana's villa is that it's secure. Our intention—' He broke off. '*My* intention when I acquired it was for it to be a luxury hotel and the perimeter security is already in place. It's been designed to keep photographers, bona fide fans and stalkers out.'

'That sounds better.'

He nodded. And then, 'Will you come?'

There was no choice. Not if she wanted to stay on Niroli. 'Yes. Yes, I will.'

'Good.'

It was as if someone had opened a floodgate to emotions she didn't know she possessed. Almost like one of those moments in a film where images flashed through a character's mind. *Mont Avellana. Her grandfather. War.* Her voice faltered. 'Will you be there?'

'Silvana will be there. You can liaise with her directly, or your people can speak to her people…' He smiled. 'Whichever suits you best.'

Isabella took a moment to assimilate that. 'I'd prefer it if you were there.' Though why she thought that would help she didn't know. Perhaps because he seemed so calm. Rocklike.

He'd started to shake his head even before she'd finished speaking. 'There's no need.'

'But—'

'No.' His eyes were shuttered. 'That isn't going to be possible. I'm sorry.'

CHAPTER FOUR

IGNORING the book on her knee, Isabella stared almost constantly from the window during the short helicopter flight from Niroli to Mont Avellana. Logically she'd not expected any dramatic change of scenery, but it still surprised her to see the almost familiar rocky cliffs and long stretches of white sandy beach.

'Equally beautiful' was how Bianca had described the islands. Isabella loosened her seat belt and tucked her novel in the bag beside her. Her friend had also told her that the people were welcoming, relaxed...

Which under normal circumstances they probably were, but Bianca didn't come to Mont Avellana as the granddaughter of a king they'd fought a war to get rid of. She came as the much-loved wife of one of their own. That would have to make a rather enormous difference to how they'd be treated.

'Your Highness...'

She looked up. Isabella snatched a quick breath and then let the air out in one calming stream. Not that it worked. Her heart was pounding from pure fear.

Please, God...help me.

A week. That was all this was. She could do that. A week

of smiling, of looking pleased to be here, and then she could go home. Back to Niroli secure in the knowledge she'd just brokered the biggest deal in their entire history. And for all his blustering her grandfather would be pleased...

She left her bag on the seat beside her and stood up. The skeleton team she'd brought with her quietly went about their business as though this really were the everyday kind of goodwill visit they were all pretending it was. There were even the usual jokes.

Isabella tried to look coolly confident as she waited for the steps to be positioned, but, inside, she felt like a little girl caught up in a vortex. *Why was she doing this?*

Did she even believe Domenic would keep his end of the bargain?

Yes, she did. She was certain he would. And that was the point. He *would* sign on that dotted line and her future would be assured. Her position in Niroli cemented...

Her bodyguard moved alongside her. 'Ready, Your Highness?'

She snapped to attention and stepped out into the familiar noise of whirring blades and the tremendous wind they created. Soft white linen trousers flicked around her legs, wind caught at hair that had been captured into a curling ponytail especially to deal with this moment. This was what she did. And she did it well.

Her Royal Highness, Princess Isabella of Niroli—reporting for duty.

Her heels made no impression on the baked hard ground as she stepped down onto Mont Avellanan soil. The first member of the Fierezza family to do so since nineteen seventy-two. She knew how newsworthy a moment that was, the message her arrival would send out across the Mediterranean.

Isabella held back her flicking ponytail and looked towards the palazzo—a seventeenth century gem, set against the backdrop of a cobalt sky and a hard lump settled in her throat.

There were no words to describe how she felt. She'd expected to feel emotional, but she'd underestimated just how emotional. Knowing her paternal grandmother had loved it here gave the place a special meaning. Made her feel as if she might cry.

'This way, Your Highness.' Her bodyguard urged her forward towards the waiting group. Tomasso's intention, no doubt, was to lead her away from open ground, but his words reminded her that her hostess was standing in the full heat of the sun. Isabella tore her eyes away from the palazzo. There'd be time later to look and think about what her family had lost.

'Come inside,' Silvana shouted above the whirr of the blades. 'Roberto and Gianni will see to your entourage. Let me get you something cool to drink.'

Isabella said nothing because she couldn't. It felt as if she were stepping off a precipice—which was pure nonsense. Nothing terrible was likely to happen to her inside the palazzo. Outside...on the streets of Mont Avellana? That was, perhaps, a different matter.

She smiled and glanced over her shoulder at Tomasso, whose eyes were darting about the enclosed grounds.

'The pool is through there.' Silvana pointed through an archway. 'It's completely private should you wish to use it during your stay. Jolanda planted trees that would screen it from any prying cameras and they've grown up beautifully.' She led the way across the lawn and up a set of wide steps.

'Jolanda?'

'Domenic's late wife. She was passionate about gardens. Always insisted he put thought and money into them before anything was done to the buildings because they'd take longer to become established.'

Isabella glanced round. Domenic's wife had been called *Jolanda*. And she'd had a hand in the design of the palazzo's gardens. Had the house fire in which she'd died been here? Her eyes wandered looking for signs of damage but the white limestone looked completely untouched.

'Domenic is waiting for us in the grand salon.'

'He's here?' She looked back at Silvana. 'I thought he was unable to…spare the time.'

'No, he's here. Against his will, maybe, but he can't resist my mother when she really wants something.' Silvana turned her head and smiled. 'Even though he likes to think otherwise, his sense of family runs like steel through his personality. He would have come out to meet you in person, but he finds the intense heat at this time of day hard to cope with.'

'I'm sure…'

'Burns survivors generally find it difficult to regulate their body temperature.'

'Yes, I know that. I'm glad he didn't feel he had to.' She was so close to asking Silvana what had happened, but she stopped herself at the last moment. It felt wrong to intrude on what was an intensely private grief.

But Domenic was here. On Mont Avellana.

Silvana led the way through the loggia with its beautifully decorated wall paintings and into a living room, painted in the deepest red.

'The *salottino rosso*,' Silvana murmured. 'I'm so proud of

this room. I think the colour is very effective. And this is the entrance hall.'

It was simply furnished. Isabella's eyes immediately took in the family emblems that ran around the top of the walls. *Her* family emblems. The palace in Niroli had similar decoration in the magnificent dining hall. She glanced across at Tomasso, keeping step beside her, wondering if he'd noticed the similarity.

'And through here…is the grand salon.'

Isabella stepped through into an immense room, decorated with what she recognised as being a late-seventeenth-century fresco and a truly magnificent Nirolian fireplace. An incongruous touch of home.

She walked towards it and ran her hand along the marble mantelpiece.

'It dates from the seventeen hundreds, I believe,' Domenic said coming up behind her.

Her pleasure at hearing his voice came as an immense surprise. Isabella spun round on her high stiletto heels. 'I think so. The shape is quite distinctive.'

'It's one of only two that survived the war.'

It was ridiculous what a difference his being here made to how she felt about being on Mont Avellana. She could feel the tension seep from her bones. 'It's a beautiful example. I'm so glad it survived.'

Domenic looked different from the last time she'd seen him. Less austere. More troubled.

'I apologise for not coming out to meet you.'

'It's extremely hot,' Isabella said quickly, 'and there was no need.'

His hand moved into a fist at the side of his body, then unclenched. Isabella noticed it and recognised it for what it was—anger.

She looked up into his strong face. He might want many things from her, but sympathy wasn't one of them. She could understand that. Though it was what she felt.

Anyone looking at Domenic Vincini would feel pity. He was a man in his mid thirties, tall, lean and toned…with the kind of natural sex appeal that came from confidence in who and what he was. A man who had driven his business to a level of unparalleled excellence.

A man who would seem to have it all.

So…it was a shame to see his face slashed down the left-hand side. Incredibly sad to know his body had been mutilated by fire.

But it was even more difficult not to feel intense pity when you realised he'd lost the people he'd loved in that tragedy.

Isabella deliberately turned away, intending to give him privacy. She couldn't change his past, but she could respect his wishes now.

Tomasso stood looking out through one of the windows. Whatever he saw obviously satisfied him because he gave her a slight nod and walked out of the salon, shutting the door quietly behind him.

'We have a great many bodyguards stay at our hotels,' Silvana remarked, 'but few seem as conscientious as yours. Most would have given a room in a place like this no more than a cursory look.'

'Tomasso's been with me six months. Before that he was assigned to Luca.' She smiled. 'I think I'm a relief.'

That and the fact that Tomasso knew she was frightened. Never spoken of, but understood all the same.

Domenic moved over towards the fan and sat down in one

of the enormous sofas that looked so tiny in the huge proportions of the room. 'Why "relief"?'

'Because I do as I'm told. I don't disappear for hours on end without telling anyone where I am.'

He gave a sudden crack of laughter. 'And Luca does?'

'Of course. You've met him. He hates being accountable to anyone and—' she shrugged her shoulders '—I suppose he doesn't feel as vulnerable.'

Silvana indicated the sofa opposite and Isabella sat down, ankles neatly crossed, hands folded loosely in her lap. She looked across at Domenic and found him watching her, a strange expression in his dark eyes. *Speculation?*

He had an odd way of doing that. Of looking deeper than any man she'd ever met before. Most were too overawed or dazzled or a combination of both to listen to what she actually said.

'Can I offer you a drink?' Silvana moved towards the doorway. 'I fancy a Caffe Shakerato since it's so hot, but we can offer you espresso, lemonade, mineral water…'

'A Caffe Shakerato would be lovely. Thank you.'

The expression in Domenic's dark eyes sharpened, but he said nothing.

Silvana's hand rested on the doorknob. 'If you'll excuse me, I'll organise that and make sure your entourage are being taken care of. Roberto and Gianni should have everything in hand, but…' She opened the door and looked a little startled to see Tomasso standing there. 'Ooh! Excuse me.'

Domenic smiled. He leant forward and picked up a wooden dice that had been left lying on the low table. He turned it over in his fingers as the door clicked shut. 'I suppose you get used to tripping over the bodyguard.'

'Eventually.'

The door clicked shut.

'But never quite?' His eyes flicked up. Dark, dark brown. 'Do you want to drink a Caffe Shakerato or are you merely being charmingly polite?'

'No, I—' She broke off as she took in the glimmer of laughter. 'I was given a choice,' she said with dignity.

'So you were,' he agreed, tossing the dice into the palm of his other hand.

'I stated my preference.'

'Did you?'

The warm understanding and soft laughter in his eyes made her smile. 'Almost.' And then she watched his smile broaden—and when he did that she stopped seeing the scars. She just felt power. A connection.

'Thank you for coming,' he said quietly.

'Did you think I wouldn't?'

'Not having met you. No.'

Which meant what?

'Once you've said you'll do something, I suspect you always do it.' He placed the dice back on the table. 'Did you encounter any opposition?'

'Yes.'

Domenic smiled. It would have been a miracle if she hadn't. She might be more amenable than Luca when it came to cooperating with her protection officers, but there had to be something steely about Isabella Fierezza for her to be here. He could only imagine how resistant King Giorgio would have been to the idea.

Strange that she could stand up to a formidable man like her grandfather and yet didn't feel able to state a preference for the everyday things of life.

The door clicked open and Silvana returned. 'Everything seems to be happening perfectly smoothly without me. I've brought my file in. I thought we could go through your itinerary—'

He stopped her. 'There's no hurry.'

'No, please.' Isabella smiled the smile she habitually hid behind. It was socially perfect and it irritated the hell out of him.

Say what you think, he urged silently. Say that you've just arrived and would like to drink your drink first. Say that you'll let her know the places you want to see in due course. *Tell her.*

'I'm not at all tired and I should like to know what you want me to do while I'm here.'

His half-sister shot him a look of triumph, but he was convinced she didn't have much to feel triumphant about.

What you saw when you were confronted by Isabella Fierezza was a consummate professional. She could be bored, tired, angry, sad, deliriously happy…and no one would suspect. There was just the tiniest chink in the façade when she'd said she felt 'vulnerable'.

And he'd noticed it—and he'd never feel quite the same about her again. In that moment, in his mind, she'd stopped being a princess of Niroli and had become a woman.

'Tonight there's a fund-raising ball at the Palazzo Razzoli.' Silvana flicked over a sheet. 'I've arranged for cars to collect us at eight-thirty.'

'Is that far from here?' Not by so much as a tremor did Isabella's well modulated voice betray any emotion. Domenic searched for a hint of something in her wide eyes. Was a fund-raising ball something she'd enjoy going to? Or not?

'Less than ten kilometres.'

Isabella nodded. There was no dangling earring to distract him. This afternoon she'd chosen pearl studs, small, round, with a luminosity that brought out the soft creaminess of her skin.

But he didn't need an earring to distract him. *She* distracted him. Simply by being. The way she spoke. The way she moved. The way she said one thing when he was certain she meant another.

His hands fisted against the fabric of the sofa. *The way she looked.* He'd have been wiser to have stayed away.

Silvana flicked over a second page. 'There's a guest list of more than five hundred, so that's an excellent start in making sure everyone knows you're here.'

'Who is going with me?'

Her eyes didn't travel in his direction. It was pitiful that he wished they had. Once upon a time he would have taken her to the charity event. *Danced with her.* He'd have been able to let his hand slide round her slight waist and pull her up close against his body.

'Silvana and her husband.' She looked at him then. Wide-eyed. Beautiful. 'They'll take great care of you,' he said, his voice husky.

His half-sister was oblivious to what he was feeling. 'It's formal evening dress. Dinner jackets. Long dresses—'

'And if you wouldn't mind wearing a tiara and a couple of insignias…' *He'd had enough.* Domenic stood up and walked over to the door, ostensibly to look for their drinks. The timing was perfect. He stepped back and let the maid come through, indicating the central table.

There was something that felt very wrong about what they were doing to Princess Isabella. Behind the sophistication and regal poise there was a woman. He wanted to tilt her face up so he could see into those beautiful eyes and read what she was really thinking.

'The tiara is fine. I never travel without one,' Isabella stated calmly into the slightly awkward silence he'd created, 'but an insignia is more of a problem.'

'I don't think anyone will expect you to wear an insignia. Dom, I—' Silvana looked up and caught the amusement in his eyes. 'Was that a joke?'

Above her head he looked across at Isabella, whose eyes were smiling. He'd not realised eyes could do that. 'Yes, a joke. It was irresistible. I'm sorry. I'm sure Isabella will be able to work out what she should wear by herself.'

'If there's anything specific you might like to tell my stylist,' Isabella said softly. 'Sometimes there's an unwritten code and I'd hate to offend anyone.'

Domenic sat back down and stretched out his legs. He believed her. A natural diplomat.

'If a hostess always wears red it would be a mistake to wear it, too.'

Particularly if you couldn't help but look better.

'Don't you think?' she said, turning to look at Silvana. Her words a gentle balm.

'I'm not aware of anything, although Imelda Bianchi does tend to wear red. Perhaps it would be better to avoid it since she's a very…fashion conscious woman. Other than that, the tickets have cost five thousand euros and everyone is looking forward to meeting you.'

The maid passed Isabella her drink and he watched her curve her long fingers round the fluted glass. The fine gold chain she wore at her wrist slipped back and blinked in the light.

'Thank you,' he said, receiving his own glass from Olivia. He sipped the creamy iced drink.

Isabella let her glass rest untried on her lap. 'And tomorrow?'

'Is Sunday.' Silvana smiled. 'I thought church. We could go to mass at the *Cattedrale di Caprera,* followed by a reception at—'

'Enough!' It was almost as though Isabella was a conquest of war and she was to be paraded around the entire island. 'Why not give Isabella a list of your suggestions? And you,' he said, looking at Isabella, 'can decide which ones seem most appropriate for what we're trying to do here.'

There was a moment's stunned silence and then Silvana shut her file with a snap. 'No problem.'

'I'm sure whatever you've arranged will be perfectly fine with me.'

Domenic stood up and walked over to the window, starring out at the piazza. Damn it! He didn't believe her. Not for a minute. She had to have a preference, some kind of *feeling* about what she was being asked to do.

He wanted to shake her with frustration. She was too perfect. Too beautiful.

And unhappy.

He turned. 'Were you serious about wanting to encourage tourism on Mont Avellana?'

Her eyes widened. 'Yes. Yes, I was. Am.'

'Then,' he said, sitting back down, 'you might like to visit some of our attractions while you're here? Rather than merely go to parties and shake the hands of the great and good?'

Isabella glanced across at Silvana, her curling ponytail swinging. 'That would be useful.'

As breakthroughs went it was small enough, but it felt good. 'Do you have any idea what you'd like to see?'

Again her ponytail swung. This time as she shook her head. 'On Niroli I work by instinct. I encourage what interests me.'

He was getting somewhere. 'So that explains the opera…?'

Isabella's face lit into a genuine smile. 'I love it. Particularly if it makes me cry.'

He nodded. Somehow that didn't come as a surprise. 'And marine life?'

'Less so.' A hand moved up to brush a stray hair from her cheek. 'But that's important, don't you think? Local festivals, traditions… I think we should treasure those.'

Domenic set his glass back down on the table. 'We might not have opera here but we do have plenty of local festivals, excellent climbing, diving, walking, scenery…'

He stopped and made sure he had eye contact. She had to hear this. Understand what he was trying to say. 'But it's enough you've come to Mont Avellana,' he said, quietly. 'Whether you ultimately decide to invest your money in projects here, you've healed a lot of hurt by being here.'

He rubbed a hand over his face. 'I hope that you'll have a pleasant stay with us.'

'Th-thank you.'

'Now, if you'll excuse me I need to speak to Toby Blake in Melbourne. If I leave it much longer he'll be asleep.'

Silvana looked as if she wanted to protest, but didn't. No doubt surprised by his outburst.

He didn't dare to look at Isabella. 'Silvana will take care of you, I know.'

He needed to get away from here, focus on work. It didn't matter what Isabella thought, or Isabella felt... It didn't matter if Isabella was happy. At least, if he were to stay sane, it shouldn't.

CHAPTER FIVE

ISABELLA pulled open the floor-to-ceiling doors that led onto the balcony and walked out to lean against the marble balustrade.

It was late—or very early, depending on your perspective—and it was hot. That still, heavy kind of airless night. It was a lot like being home on Niroli.

Except there was silence. And she loved that. After the bustle of the charity ball, silence was the most perfect thing.

It had been a long, long evening. She'd smiled, she'd laughed—she'd done everything anyone could have reasonably expected of her… In fact, everything she always did.

'Are you sure you don't want any help with your dress or hair, Your Highness?'

Isabella turned and walked back into the bedroom, resting her hand on one of the posts of the enormous four-poster bed. 'I can manage by myself, thank you, Mia. It's a simple enough dress.'

Her stylist smiled. 'Good night, then, Your Highness.'

'Good night.' Isabella watched her leave and sat down on the edge of the bed. She wasn't a fool. When her normally meticulous stylist was prepared to let her take care of her own clothes there must be a strong reason. Particularly when she'd sat up to nearly three in the morning for her to come back to the palazzo.

Isabella smiled. She hadn't missed the look that had passed between Mia and Tomasso. They were in love. She was sure of it. And that meant there'd be more changes for her in the near future. Tomasso would be taken off her staff and she'd have another Chief of Security watching her every move.

But, to look on the bright side, at least this one hadn't fallen in love with her. Isabella eased her feet out of her high sandals and wriggled her toes, before padding back across to the open doors.

That was where she wanted to be. Outside. Breathing in real air and listening to nothing. If she really followed her inclination she'd put on her swimming costume and go for a swim.

No! If she really followed her inclination she wouldn't bother with the swimming costume. Just skin and cool water. That would be perfect.

And completely inappropriate for a woman like her.

The palazzo's security had won high praise from Tomasso, but it was never worth taking the chance. Some exceptionally determined photographer would find a way of circumventing it.

As her mother had always said, being a princess brought both privilege and responsibility. And she was a very good princess. Day in, day out, that was what she did.

She walked back through and pulled the curtains across. Unlike other members of her family who took the privileges and left the responsibilities. Marco. Luca. Though to be fair, neither Alex or Luca had ever expected or wanted to be king.

And Marco had fallen in love. Deep down, wasn't that what she wanted for herself?

But all that left her precisely where? Everything was shifting about so much she wasn't sure where she fitted in any more.

Isabella glanced back over at the balcony. It was so hot.

And she was so restless. With sudden decisiveness she picked up her sandals off the bed and walked barefoot out of the bedroom and along the wide landing towards the staircase.

The first hint she wasn't alone came from the glimmer reflected in the hall mirror. Like a moth she followed it—and found a lamp left alight in the beautiful sitting room. She moved over to switch it off and noticed the doors had been left open to the *terrazzo*.

Holding her sandals with one finger, she moved to look out. Somehow it wasn't a surprise to see Domenic Vincini sitting there. Alone. Still as an image in a photograph. And sad.

Isabella hesitated in the doorway for a moment, wondering whether she ought to go quietly back up to her room. He was staring out across the darkened gardens, his hand loosely wrapped around a half-empty wineglass, which told her he must have been there sometime.

The decision not to intrude was taken away from her. He looked up, his face half in shadow. 'Isabella!'

She stepped out into the moonlight. 'I'm sorry. Am I disturbing you?'

'No. I'm…' Domenic stood up and he gestured towards the still-almost-full bottle of wine on the table.

She nodded. 'Yes, I see.'

He set his glass down on the table. 'Is there anything you need? Is your room comfortable? I—'

'It's lovely.' Isabella tentatively walked forward, her sandals in one hand and the fabric of her long skirt caught up in the other. 'I thought I'd get some air. It's so hot and I don't feel like sleeping yet.'

'Parties don't exhaust you?'

Her smile twisted. 'Some peace would be nice.'

Domenic ran a hand around the back of his neck. 'Would you like to join me?'

The invitation seemed wrung from him, but Isabella nodded. 'I'd like that. Thank you.'

In fact, she'd like that very much. Their dinner together had been like an oasis in a life that felt increasingly difficult.

Why was that? Nothing amazing had happened. He'd talked. She'd talked. But it had all felt so easy. There'd been no sense of having to watch what she said for fear it would end up twisted.

After an evening like tonight she really needed that. Constant scrutiny and the need to watch everything you said had a way of wearing you down.

She sat down on the second wrought iron seat and took a deep breath. The air was rich and spicy with the scent of orange blossom. So like home. She'd merely exchanged a secluded balcony for a wide *terrazzo*. Solitude for company.

'I'll fetch a second glass.'

'No, I…' If there'd been time she'd have stopped him, but he'd turned away almost immediately and didn't hear her.

Isabella sat back in her chair. It was so quiet. She could get used to this. Her suite of rooms within the Villa Berlusconi were her private sanctuary, but there was always a hubbub of noise until the early hours.

She smiled wryly in the darkness. She had to take some responsibility for that. Without her active encouragement there probably wouldn't be the plethora of smart cafés and street performances.

But here the silence was so complete she could almost hear the thump of her heartbeat. And it was lovely.

'I would have brought the water in something more elegant, but I couldn't find anything suitable.'

Isabella turned to see Domenic carrying a large earthenware jug, the kind that was more likely to hold flowers.

'There must be something better in one of the cupboards, but I haven't the first idea where to look. To be honest I did well to find the glasses.'

She felt a bubble of laughter form in the pit of her stomach. 'How long is it since you were last here?' she asked as he set the pitcher down on the table and then the glass.

'A year.' He sat down. 'I find it difficult to come back.'

'To the palazzo?'

He shook his head. 'Mont Avellana. I love it and hate it here in pretty much equal measure. I only come when I really have to.'

Isabella stashed her sandals beneath her chair and wiggled her toes. 'Because of the fire?'

She watched the convulsive movement of his throat, so near the damaged skin that ran its length.

'Yes, the fire.'

Pain ripped through his voice and Isabella wished she'd not spoken without thinking. Of course he'd want to be as far away as possible from the place that had taken everything he valued most. 'Do you need to come?'

'Yes and no. Every year I say I won't, but then I change my mind. It's my father's birthday in a few days' time. Once a year he likes to have his entire family around him—sons, daughters, grandchildren… It seems little enough to ask.'

But one of those grandchildren would be missing. Domenic's child. So that was what Silvana had meant when she'd said family was 'like steel running through him'. He would come, every year, even though it hurt him to do so.

Domenic continued. 'I'll fly back to Rome the day after. Visit over for another year.'

Which would leave her alone here. It didn't help to remember that was only what she'd expected when she'd first arrived.

'Wine or water?' He held up the bottle of wine. 'This is imported. Sardinian. Sella & Mosca Alghero "Le Arenarie". You might like it. It's light, a little lemony. Not as dry as your Porto Castellante Blanco.'

Isabella held out her glass. 'Please.' He poured some wine into her glass and she took a tentative sip. 'It's nice,' she said politely.

He laughed, a sudden bark. 'Why do you do that?'

'What?'

'Say what you think I want you to say, rather what you really think.'

'I don't—'

His right eyebrow shot up.

'Maybe. Sometimes,' she said in response. 'It's a habit.'

'Tip it away if you'd prefer water.'

'No, I'll drink it,' she said, resting her hand on her glass as though she thought he might take it from her. 'My sister would never forgive me if I did anything as sacrilegious as throw it away. Do you know how much love is lavished on grapes?'

'No.'

'More than many parents give to their children.' She took another cautious sip. 'This isn't too bad.'

'Damned with faint praise.' Domenic lifted his own glass, catching sight of his rolled up shirt sleeve. He put his glass down again and went to unroll it.

The sudden movement drew her eyes to the puckered and discoloured skin on his forearm. 'Don't. Please.'

His hand hesitated.

'Not on my account, anyway,' she said quietly and deliberately turned her face away to look out across the garden. She lifted her head back to catch the gentle night-time breeze on her face.

'Is saying the socially preferable thing a learnt habit or are you a natural pleaser?'

She turned her head to look at him, glad to see he'd left his sleeve rolled up. The skin on his arm was dark brown and wrinkled to a point midway down his forearm. But his hands were beautiful. Strong, sculptural, unblemished in any way.

'It's a long story,' she said with a shake of her head.

'I'm not going anywhere.'

She shook her head again. To explain that would be to explain the dynamics of her family and that was private. Too private to share, however lovely a garden and cooling the night breeze.

However fabulous a listener the man she was with happened to be.

He seemed to recognise that because he smiled and it occurred to her that it wasn't only his hands that were beautiful. 'How was it tonight?'

'At the ball?'

He nodded.

'Truthfully?'

'Of course.'

'Well…' She smiled and set her glass down on the table. 'I'm assuming you don't want fashion details…'

'Er…not particularly.'

'Though you might be interested to know Imelda Bianchi did wear red.'

'Which made your blue the perfect choice.'

Socially and aesthetically perfect. Domenic took another sip of wine and let the tang of lemon bite against his tongue.

No woman should look as beautiful as Isabella. Her hair was a million shades of corn and gold. Warm. Rich. Stunning. And she, or her stylist, had clipped her heavy curls back off her face with a barrette of pale blue gemstones set on wires to look like dancing cornflowers. The tiniest sapphire drops hung in her ears, nothing at her neck or on her wrist. Simple. Unaffected. And she'd have made every other woman look like an overdecorated Christmas tree.

'It's always a good idea to know in advance what your hostess is likely to wear. I learnt that very early on in my career.' Isabella toyed with her wineglass. 'Fashion among women is a competitive business.'

'You make it sound like war.'

She looked up. 'It's gamesmanship. And some of it comes from men, I think. "My wife is more attractive than your wife", "I can afford to buy my wife better jewels".' She wrinkled her nose. 'That kind of thing.'

Isabella Fierezza was a cynic. The next time he saw her smiling from a magazine cover he'd know what was really going on behind those amber-flecked eyes.

Domenic sat forward to refill his glass. 'What did you think of the Palazzo Razzoli?'

'Now that was beautiful. And Vittore and Imelda had clearly gone to a lot of effort and expense to make it a wonderful evening. They'd even laid a mirrored dance floor across the ballroom.'

'Tacky.'

She laughed and he found he loved to hear it. 'Well… tricky anyway. It was considered spectacular, but I gave it a wide birth. There are some photographs of me I don't want circulating on the World Wide Web.'

'Where there many photographers there?'

'Lots. I shouldn't think there'll be anyone on Mont Avellana who won't know I'm here by the end of the weekend.'

'Excellent.'

'Mission accomplished,' she said lightly.

And it was, so why did he feel as if he'd stolen something from her?

'Is it true that the Bianchis were once a noble family?'

He almost choked on his wine. 'Is that what he told you? Vittore's grandfather was a mountain shepherd.'

'Imelda did. Or implied it.' She frowned. 'I wish people didn't feel they had to do that.'

'She wanted to impress you, I suppose,' he said, watching her over the rim of his glass. 'Why does it bother you so much?'

'It implies that they think that matters to me.'

He smiled. Isabella was nothing like the woman he'd thought she was. He'd love it if he could introduce her to his father. Would she be prepared to meet him? An elderly republican and the granddaughter of the man he'd helped depose?

He shook his head. It wouldn't be right to put her in that kind of an awkward position. But he was fairly sure they'd like each other. His father would certainly love her. Aside from anything else he knew a beautiful woman when he saw one.

'I also wish she hadn't shown me the bullet holes in the courtyard wall—'

Domenic sat forward. 'She didn't!'

'Apparently it was caught in crossfire in the August of nineteen seventy-two and Vittore thinks it should be kept for posterity. Some kind of warning against human frailty, I believe.'

Her eyes twinkled with suppressed amusement and Domenic felt himself relax back in his chair. 'And what did you say?'

'That it was always wise to remember the mistakes of the past.'

The consummate professional. His finger stroked around the rim of his glass. 'Where was Silvana when all this was happening?'

Isabella let the laughter out. 'Two feet away from me and she performed an excellent rescue mission. Smooth, swift and practically undetectable.'

He laughed.

'Your sister is very lovely.'

'You didn't grow up with her.'

'Neither did you I hear.' Isabella looked up at him with a slanting expression.

'Not until I turned fifteen. No.'

'Silvana told me.'

How much had she told her? He didn't want Isabella's view of him distorted by other people's gossip, malicious or otherwise.

A memory speared into his head, fresh and clear—and for the first time it didn't hurt him to remember. Jolanda had laughed up at him. Teasing. *'Women talk, Dom. Of course I know if you so much as smile at another woman.'* He'd known then that he never would smile at another woman because he'd found the one he'd wanted.

And they'd been happy together. It was all too easy to forget that and simply remember the grief that had come later.

'Did she tell you why?'

'No. I merely said something about you two being close and she said it was surprising since you hadn't lived with them until you were fifteen.'

Ah.

'I'm sorry. I didn't mean to pry.'

'It's no secret.' He sipped his wine. 'My mother grew up on Niroli. Then at eighteen, she went to Rome to study and met my father. After a very swift romance they married and she came to live on Mont Avellana. I think they were reasonably happy for the first couple of years, until my father's politics got in the way.'

'I'm sorry.'

'It's not your fault.' He smiled. 'They can take full responsibility for their own mistakes. I was a "sticking plaster" baby, I think, born to keep a marriage together, but in the end my mother left and took me to London.'

'Did she marry again?'

Domenic shook his head. 'She was a good Catholic girl and felt she'd failed her vows. Lived the rest of her life between a rock and a hard place.'

Why was he telling her this? The last person he'd told any of this to was Jolanda. It was simply that he wanted Isabella to understand something about his relationship with his family. And God only knew why that was.

He shifted in his seat. 'She died when I was fifteen and I came back to live with my father and his new family. My father is a bad Catholic and had no such scruples in creating one.'

'Did you know him well?'

'Not then. I was uprooted and landed unceremoniously on his doorstop. Fortunately my stepmother is a rather special woman.'

Isabella said something under her breath. He smiled, almost sure she'd sworn.

'I thought I'd had it tough.'

Surprisingly it hadn't felt so tough, even at the time. And it certainly wasn't when viewed through what had happened to him since. He took a sip of his wine. 'What happened to you?'

'Boarding school. Nothing in comparison to you, but I hated it. I'd never been away from home before and I missed my mother. I only started to settle and make some friends after my sister was born. The fact that she wasn't the "spare" heir everyone was hoping for made me feel better.'

The poor little rich girl. No doubt that was where some of her vulnerability stemmed from. Curious that someone as beautiful as Isabella Fierezza should carry with her a feeling of not being quite good enough.

'And then Rosa turned out to be the cutest baby with a halo of dark curls.'

'So you forgave her for being born?'

'Naturally. I drew her hundreds of pictures to decorate her nursery because I was worried she'd forget who I was.'

'And became firm friends.'

She hesitated. 'Eventually. Seven years is a lot between children. Since my parents' accident we've been much closer, though it has to be by e-mail. Rosa works in New Zealand.'

'I'd heard that.'

'It's such a long way away.' Isabella rubbed at her arms. 'It must be incredibly late. What time is it?'

'Half past four. Just after.'

'I'd better try and get some sleep. I've got mass to go to in the morning.'

'Only if you want to.'

Isabella smiled and shook her head. 'That's not how this game is played,' she said, pushing her chair back.

His hand snaked out and stopped her with a light touch. 'I meant what I said earlier. It's enough you're here.'

She looked slightly shocked, a suspicion of a blush along her cheekbones. 'Thank you.'

'I mean it. Just by being here you'll have raised the profile of Mont Avellana.'

Isabella gave a choking laugh. 'It's what I do.'

Yes, it was. And she did it well. But where did that leave time for Isabella Fierezza the woman? When did she ever do something because it was fun?

Domenic put down his glass. 'Come with me. I've got something I'd like you to see.'

He stood up.

'What?'

'The sunrise. There's no point staying up until morning if you miss the best part of the day.'

'See the sunrise?'

'Come and see. It's particularly beautiful from the gardens.'

Could she? 'I'd like that. If you're sure Silvana won't mind if I'm fit for nothing in the morning.'

'She won't mind.'

Why did an innocent thing like staying up all night and watching the day begin feel a little wicked? Isabella caught the flash of his smile and reached down for her sandals.

'Leave them. You won't need them. It's across the lawn.'

Barefoot. In an evening dress. *With a man who made her feel special.*

Isabella glanced sideways up at him. Standing to his right you couldn't even see the scars. Dressed in loose-fitting linen trousers and a white T-shirt covered with an open shirt, he looked relaxed and sexy. A little dangerous.

And they were going to watch the sunrise together.

She felt happy. Everything seemed brighter. The moon

shone that little bit stronger. Scents in the air were intensified. The grass felt softer and looked greener.

'Do you often stay up all night and watch the sunrise?'

'I often stay up until the early hours. It's cooler at night and I like it. And without air-conditioning it becomes even more appealing.' He turned his head towards her and she caught sight of the scars down his face. 'But I don't deliberately stay up to see the sunrise any more.'

The expression in his eyes made her feel a little breathless. 'Why?'

'Because they can't be watched alone.'

Her stomach rolled over. 'I suppose that's true.' Although that was exactly what she did do. Camera in hand, she loved to see the day begin. But he was right—it made you feel lonely when there was no one to share that kind of breathtaking beauty with.

Domenic led her through the archway and along the side of an impressive pool, all the more stunning because of the view from it. One side was shielded by the trees Silvana had mentioned. The other was a huge mass of barely undulating sea. Miles and miles. A strange, dark and eerily beautiful world.

'Will you ruin your dress if you sit on the grass?'

'I shouldn't think so. It's so dry.' *And she didn't care*. This felt a little like magic. As though she'd walked into one of the films she loved to watch.

She settled herself comfortably and stretched out her legs, one foot resting across the top of the other.

Domenic sat beside her. 'If we'd planned this better we should have brought rugs to sit on. Jolanda and I used to bring out cappuccinos and doughnuts and make it an early breakfast.'

'Here?' Isabella glanced up at the trees. The trees his late wife had planted but not lived to see grow.

He shook his head. 'We had a small balcony. Barely room for a table and a couple of chairs. In the beginning. All this came later.'

'You must miss her.'

'Every day.' His voice was low. 'I miss them both.'

Isabella's hand felt the softness of the grass beside her. She was here because they couldn't be.

And it was too awful to talk about why they weren't here.

'Look.' Domenic pointed out to sea. 'He'll have been out all night.'

She followed the line of his finger and there, on the horizon, was a white fishing boat. Isabella pulled her knees up to her chest and kept watching. She could feel the breeze that came off the sea tug at her hair, taste the salt on her lips.

It felt as if everything were waiting, trembling on the brink of something. First she heard a lone gull, and then slowly it was joined by other birds. Isabella held her breath. And still it wasn't morning.

Just the two of them. No one was watching. There was no reason to be here but that they wanted to be.

'What was Jolanda like?' she asked quietly, almost too quietly to be heard although she knew he had. She felt him tense beside her.

'She was…' Domenic raised a hand to shield his face. 'She was fun.' He pulled the air into his lungs and continued. 'She had a way of making the little things seem special. We could do absolutely nothing and I'd feel like I'd had the best time.'

Isabella looked back out to sea. High in the sky the feathery cirrus clouds had turned all shades of pink. It was dramatic and it was beautiful, but she scarcely saw it.

That was what she wanted for herself. Someone who, when it was all over, would sit there and say that she'd made the world a better place for them.

'I miss being part of her life. I miss the dreams we had together.' He looked at her. 'And I wonder all the time what life would have been like if they hadn't died. Our daughter would have been five in October.'

Isabella felt the lump in her throat stopping her ability to swallow. And she felt ashamed. She'd allowed self-pity to colour her life and yet she had nothing to be unhappy about. Not in the larger scheme of things.

So her life wasn't perfect. Whose was?

'What was your daughter's name?'

'Felice.' His voice deepened and the emotion he was feeling ripped through her. 'Felice Alisa.'

Oh, God. Isabella couldn't do this. It hurt too much to think about what had happened to him. To them.

One single teardrop spilled out and ran down her face, leaving a glistening trail. How did he bear it? How could he go on day after day after day…?

Then she felt a hand rest gently on top of hers. His. Warm. Comforting. Isabella looked up, her eyes glistening.

'Thank you for asking the question and for listening to the answer.'

Another tear tipped over and spilled down the path the first had made.

'No one lets me talk about them.' Domenic raised a hand and gently brushed away the tears on her face. 'And if I don't talk about them I'm scared I'll forget how incredible they were. How lucky I was to have them in my life.'

'I'm sorry you lost them,' she said, her voice broken. There was nothing she could say that would make it better. Nothing that could put it right.

Domenic lifted her hand from the grass and cradled it in his lap, his fingers stroking the length of her palm. Isabella shivered and he moved to wrap an arm around her.

Two lonely people watching the sunrise.

It was too precious to spoil with words. The simple act of holding each other was enough. More than enough.

Then the first suspicion of orange filtered into the sky, gradually spreading. Brighter. Stronger. It was a huge shame she didn't have her camera with her, but she wouldn't have traded this moment for anything.

Isabella looked up at Domenic's profile and noticed the hint of stubble. It would be easy to reach up and touch the roughness of his face, feel the bristles against her fingers. He was so close she could feel his chest move when he took a breath. It was the first time in almost a decade someone had held her. Just held her.

'We'd better get back,' he said against her hair.

Isabella closed her eyes and tried to imprint on her memory how wonderful this felt. *She didn't want to go back.*

'I'll talk to Silvana and tell her you need sleep more than mass today.'

'I don't think I could risk closing my eyes in prayer,' she said, allowing him to pull her to her feet. 'I'm not sure a snoring ambassador of peace and tolerance would be quite as effective.'

'Perhaps not.' He kept hold of her hand as they walked across the grass back to the *terrazzo*. Once there, he released it and Isabella bent to pick up her sandals.

'Isabella?'

She turned, clutching her sandals against her waist. 'Yes?'

'My family's having Sunday lunch together. Would you care to join us?'

And not go to the afternoon reception that had been pencilled in?

She looked at his face, impassive but for the tiny pulse beating in his cheek.

'If you'd prefer not to I'd completely understand. My father's mellowed over the years, but his politics—'

'I'd love to. Thank you.' Then she stepped forward and pressed a light kiss on his scarred cheek.

CHAPTER SIX

ISABELLA had kissed him on the cheek.

Watching her with the sunlight glinting on her hair, it was difficult to believe it had happened. God only knew how much that simple gesture had meant to him. Acceptance. Friendship. At least that was what he chose to believe.

Domenic reached a hand up and ran his fingers down his ravaged face, reminding himself that she could only have done it out of pity. She'd hardly have been overcome by passion.

Beauty and the beast.

Domenic smiled. He wasn't holding his breath for that kind of happy ending. He didn't even want it. He reached out and picked up a fig from the platter in front of him. He'd had his chance at happiness. It had been wonderful, but now it was over.

Everyone said that time was a great healer, but everyone didn't know what they were talking about. Time passed. That was all. Nothing changed. Every morning he woke up and the realisation seeped through him that he was alone.

Jolanda was still dead. Felice would never be older in his mind than the nine months she'd been when fire had ripped through their home. To try and recreate what he'd already had would be a betrayal of what he'd felt for them.

Leastways that was what he wanted to believe he felt. Thinking that would make it easier to accept he'd never have that kind of happiness again. Domenic moved back further under the shade of the pine, his skin prickling with the heat. He'd never have a woman like Isabella Fierezza look at him with any kind of desire.

Silvana slid alongside him. 'She's lovely.'

'Who?'

His half-sister bit into an almond sweet. 'The woman you're watching.' She looked up, finishing her *sospiri d'orani*. 'You know, you do go for very up-market women. First Jolanda, now…'

Domenic dragged a hand round the back of his neck. If Silvana had noticed how fascinated he was by Isabella, then he could be certain his stepmother had done the same. He glanced over to where she was seated, grandchildren around her. She looked up and smiled. Then they both looked at Isabella.

For a moment. That was all he'd allow himself. But he could hear her voice. He didn't need to look at Isabella to know how her hands moved when she was trying to explain something, or how her eyes sparkled when she found something funny.

It was a mistake to have brought her here. It had been the impulse of the moment. But now, whenever he returned, he'd know what it felt like to see her among the people he loved.

He'd wanted to show her the real Mont Avellana. The inner world. The world that people who came searching for white sand and warm sea would never experience. But more than that, he wanted her to have a memory that was something other than the chink of crystal and the flash of diamonds.

And she seemed to love it. He'd wondered how a princess

of Niroli would manage when her wine came in a rustic pitcher and her food was simple. But nothing, it seemed, fazed Isabella.

She'd looked at the huge platter of suckling pig and Mont Avellanan veal, both cooked in the old stone oven in the backyard, and had asked about the wood they'd used in the cooking of it. In one fell stroke she'd won another army of admirers as they'd fiercely contested the use of sumac, moving on to consider the merits of fennel on a grill when cooking sea bass.

His father was in a particularly expansive mood, but she seemed able to take him in her stride. Just as easily as she had the three generations of Vincini family seated along the series of rustic tables. Not by so much as a flicker did she appear anything other than delighted to be where she was and talking to the people around her.

It was a rare gift.

And he was lying.

It wasn't a mistake to have brought her here. Nor had it been the impulse of the moment. It had been the impulse of many moments. Beginning when he'd switched on his monitor and seen her look directly into the camera. She'd known she was being watched. And he'd known she didn't like it but would stay as long as it took to get what she wanted.

Isabella was here because he liked her. When she looked at him she seemed to see him and not the scars. She looked him in the eye and he felt good about himself.

And when he looked at her he saw goodness. And loneliness. He saw that, too. Loneliness that reached in and touched him, forging an unexpected bond.

His eyes pulled round to look at her again—because he

couldn't help it. Honey-gold curls captured in a low ponytail by a wide band of red, small studs in her earlobes and a cotton sundress that made her look fresh and cool despite the searing heat.

She was a public relations dream. Exactly what he'd told her he wanted. A woman who could do something for Mont Avellana in exchange for what he could give to Niroli. But everything was changing for him…

His father moved his hand in a sweeping motion. 'The whole notion of monarchy is outmoded.'

'You might not like it, but that doesn't make it outmoded,' she said in her husky voice that made his body heat in a way that had nothing to do with weather. 'How many times have you seen something done purely for expediency in the short term because the politician knows they won't be there to be accountable for that decision even five years later?'

'Democracy may be flawed, but it is a better system than leadership awarded by virtue of birth. What right have you to rule over other people?'

'Personally? None. I'm a victim of primogeniture,' she said, reaching for a fig. 'As a woman in a family of so many men I'm unlikely to become the Queen of Niroli but, if it were my birthright, I'd aim to find the middle ground between the two systems. Take the best of both.'

His father made a noise that was suspiciously like a grunt. 'But your wealth isn't earned.'

If Isabella needed any help from him he'd have given it, but Domenic knew from her slanting smile that she was in complete control. The steely core he'd always known she possessed was shining in his vocally aggressive family. And his father was mesmerised by her as he'd known he would be.

'And the land you own?' She glanced around at the stone villa set against a mountain backdrop. 'Isn't this all inherited?' She smiled at his father's silence and Domenic smiled to see it. 'We're all born to different circumstances. I believe our responsibility is to live as best we can. We should make the most of the opportunities we've been given.'

Not at all the woman he'd first thought she was.

Domenic met his stepmother's eyes and read the compassion in them. They both knew Isabella Fierezza would never contemplate a man like him. It didn't matter how good her hand had felt in his. How soft her skin. Or that he knew what her lips felt like against his cheek. He pushed back his chair. 'It's too hot for me now. I'm going to sit under the pergola.'

Silvana looked up. 'I'll come and keep you company.'

'There's no need.' Domenic glanced across at his stepmother. 'If Princess Isabella needs me…'

Lucetta nodded. And he knew she understood. Her hand fell on her eldest grandson's head. Domenic pulled his hand across his face. Lucetta understood that, too. There was a child missing. And she'd always be missing. Best he remembered that before he started to hanker after a romantic dream.

Domenic was exactly where Silvana had said he'd be. Isabella pushed the baby onto one hip and held onto the doorframe so she didn't slip on the high step down.

'What are you reading?' she asked, walking beneath the vine covered pergola.

He turned at her voice, unguarded, and for that second she could see…something that made her feel breathless. Then it was gone. He held up his novel.

She forced a smile. 'Blood and guts.'

'You've read it?'

'I've heard it talked about. I've been asked to take Carlo to find somewhere cool. The sun's so hot.'

He turned his book over so that it rested on the seat beside him. 'By who?'

'Silvana,' she said, her hand moving to hold Carlo's bare foot. 'She said I'd find you here.'

He nodded, but said nothing as she sat in the chair opposite. 'Are you feeling all right?'

'Nothing I'm not used to,' he said, running a hand across his face.

Isabella's eyes flicked to the darkened skin showing starkly against the white of his loose shirt. No, she supposed it wasn't. Hiding from the scorching heat of high summer would be part and parcel of his experience.

She settled Carlo across her lap and gave him her finger to hold. He pulled it firmly against his mouth and rooted as though he were at a breast. 'He's just been fed and your cousin says he should sleep now.'

'He looks tired.'

'Yes, but still hungry.' She looked up suddenly and caught him watching them, the expression in his eyes unbearably sad. It was gone in an instant. Isabella glanced down at the baby cradled against her as a new thought occurred to her.

This must be difficult for him. 'Would you rather we sat somewhere else?'

'No.' He shifted in his seat. 'It's cool here and Carlo will sleep.'

Which wasn't what she'd meant and he knew it. Isabella bit her lip and let the silence stretch out between them. She listened to the chirruping cicadas in the bushes, wishing she'd taken Carlo somewhere else. She might be fighting the deep seated ache for a baby of her own, but he was missing Felice. She should have thought.

Domenic moved to pick up his book again, but didn't. His fingers rested against the spine. 'Has my father offended you at all?'

'Of course not. Why?'

His smile twisted. 'He isn't particularly good at seeing anyone's point of view but his own.'

'Who is?' Isabella watched as Carlo's eyes gently closed, his little round face completely sated. He was so lovely. 'Your father reminds me of my grandfather a little. They probably don't have an opinion in common, but they have the same innate certainty they're right.'

'You sound fond of him.'

'Grandfather?' She looked up. 'Yes, I am. He's honestly one of the most remarkable men I've ever met. I suppose you don't have a particularly high opinion of him...'

His mouth quirked and she didn't need him to say anything. It wasn't surprising that someone who'd been born on Mont Avellana would feel that way. Perhaps his treatment of what he'd seen as a satellite island hadn't been fair.

'But he's my grandfather.'

'Of course.'

'And I love him.' Isabella twisted one of Carlo's dark curls in her fingers. 'I've seen a different side of him. Did you know he can make a paper aeroplane that can fly across the entire dining hall? Or that he can recite Wordsworth in the most perfect English accent? And that he carries a picture of my grandmother with him everywhere he goes, even though she's been dead more years than she was alive?'

Domenic smiled. 'No.'

'I don't think everything he's done has been right, but I do believe he's done them honestly. And I know he loves Niroli.'

'And that's all that matters?'

'It's important if you happen to be the sovereign of it, don't you think?' Her hand moved to rest on Carlo's tummy and she felt his chest move up and down. 'And the last two years have been an incredibly painful and difficult time for him.'

'I can imagine.'

She looked up. There were probably few men on earth who could truly empathise. First her grandfather had lost the wife he loved, then a grandson and, finally, both sons.

'Difficult for you, too.'

Isabella slid her finger into Carlo's limp hand. She loved the feel of his tiny fingers. So perfect. So small. 'Sometimes I don't believe it's happened. My father was such an experienced sailor. I keep thinking it's all been a stupid mistake and everything will go back to the way it was…' She stopped herself, suddenly aware of what she was saying—and to whom.

'I know that feeling.'

'I'm sorry, I—'

'Were you close to your parents?'

She rushed to answer him. 'Yes. Though my father was…very private and difficult to know. At least with me.'

And he'd been completely dominated by his own father. That was the one thing that had constantly annoyed her about him.

'But he would have made a good king, I think.'

'And your mother?'

'Would have been a charming and beautiful consort.'

Domenic smiled, his face becoming instantly softer.

'She was my best friend.' Warm memories crowded round

her, comforting her as they always did. Though now there was the nip of pain when she thought about how much it would have meant to her mother to have known her second son was alive and happy.

A surgeon. She'd have been proud of that. Proud of Alex's decision to continue with a life that made him happy. Hopeful of grandchildren and a chance to play a meaningful part in his life.

'Is she why you decided to settle on Niroli?' Domenic asked, startling her out of her thoughts.

Isabella gave a shocked laugh. 'No. Though she was what made it bearable. In the first couple of years anyway, before I found something I could do.'

'You didn't want to come back?'

She shook her head. 'I wanted to do a degree in English and Spanish, but I needed my grandfather's permission.'

'And he refused?'

Sitting there under a shady vine, a warm little body heavy in her arms, it was easy to forget how angry she'd been.

'What did your parents do?'

'Nothing. It wasn't their decision to make. I suppose that's what I was trying to say to your father. You have to live as well as you can within the circumstances you find yourself. My mother taught me that. She was the most gracious woman.'

Carlo snuffled and Isabella looked down with a smile. This was what she wanted. If she could choose. A family of her own. People to love and who would love her. Maybe if she'd had more courage at nineteen she'd have had that now.

'I had to have the king's permission to live anywhere but Niroli. And my grandfather didn't give it.'

A frown snapped across Domenic's head. 'Why?'

'Because he believed it wasn't necessary to educate women to the same standard as men. His own marriages were arranged, my parents' all but. I think he honestly believed that would be my future.'

'Marriage to a European prince?'

Isabella's fingers buried themselves in Carlo's soft curls. 'Fifty years ago that would have been my lot, but princes are more inclined to marry for love than bloodlines.'

'Are you disappointed?'

'Having now met most of the eligible princes across Europe, I don't think so.' She looked up and smiled. 'But I was very angry Marco had permission to live in London when I was refused it.'

'I can see why.'

Isabella felt Domenic's anger on her behalf. 'I was silly though. I could have defied him and done exactly what I wanted. The only power he has over me is my place in the succession, and since my cousins will inherit ahead of me…'

Her tone must have given away more than she'd intended. 'A victim of primogeniture.'

She smiled at the echo of her own words. 'Years ago I used to try and argue it out with my father, but he only ever said that it was the way it was and there was nothing to discuss.'

'Did he want you to marry a nameless prince?'

'He never expressed an opinion other than to tell me my face would be my fortune.'

Her father was a quiet voice at the back of her head that undermined everything she tried to do. It didn't matter how hard she worked, how much she achieved, his voice was still in her head telling her that her value was entirely based on her ability to look 'pretty'.

Even now. Two years after his death.

And it was even worse now because he wasn't alive for her to show him how wrong he'd been.

'Isabella?'

'I'm here.' She looked round at Lucetta's voice.

The older lady stood in the doorway, her round face thoughtful as she watched them. 'Is Carlo asleep?'

'Soundly.'

'And snoring,' Domenic added.

Isabella smiled down at him, loving the little grunting noise he made.

'Then come and lay him down inside. You'll make yourself too hot if you have to sit and hold him all the time he's sleeping. Silvana shouldn't have asked you to do this. Come.' Lucetta encouraged her to come in. 'We keep a cot up in the little bedroom. And we can put a fan on him to keep him cooler.'

Reluctantly Isabella walked inside and through into a narrow, oblong room. A simple wooden cot was against the far wall, already made up and waiting. Lucetta rested her plump hand on the carved end. 'My father made this for my eldest son.'

'It's lovely.' Isabella carefully laid Carlo on his back, slightly disappointed when his eyes didn't open in protest.

'He was a talented carpenter. He also made us the most beautiful rocking horse, but that was lost in the fire at Domenic's home.'

Isabella looked round.

'Has he told you about the fire?'

'A little.' Then, 'No. Not really.' Not about the fire. He'd spoken about Jolanda. About Felice. But not about the day itself. Nothing about how he'd got his scars.

'Come with me. I want to show you something.'

Isabella glanced back at the sleeping baby and then followed Domenic's stepmother into her cosily furnished sitting room. It was a room full of nick-nacks. Tiny crucifixes mingled with homemade cards and mismatched photo frames.

'Now…' Lucetta walked towards a table in the corner and reached towards the back, selecting a photograph standing in a black lacquered frame. 'This one is of Domenic taken five years ago.'

For a moment she didn't realise the significance of what Lucetta had said. But then her eyes travelled to the image and she looked back up at Domenic's stepmother. She was standing with her hand clutching at the small cross at her neck.

Isabella looked back down at the photograph. Domenic before the scars. Before the fire. Before tragedy had taken away the laughter.

'And this is another one. Of him with Jolanda,' she said, passing across a second picture, this time in a red plastic frame. 'That was taken the year before she got pregnant with Felice.'

Isabella held one in each hand. Jolanda had been small and dark. Elfin features surrounded by a cloud of black hair. Laughing.

And Domenic had been one of the most charismatically good-looking men she'd ever seen. Strong, handsome and supremely confident.

She concentrated on the smooth skin that stretched over a tanned face. The short-sleeved T-shirt that showed the arms of a sportsman. The sexy glint in his eyes.

A compelling and supremely attractive man.

How much harder did that make the scarring to deal with? To look in the mirror and see someone he didn't recognise? To be treated differently?

Isabella looked back up at Lucetta. 'What did happen?'

Lucetta took the photographs from her listless fingers and looked at them. 'Fires are not that uncommon here. The smallest spark will set it off during the summer months.'

She placed them back on the table. 'The fire started in the middle of the day. No one really knows why exactly. Jolanda and little Felice must have been asleep because no one raised the alarm until the fire had pretty much taken hold.'

Isabella felt as though someone had reached inside her and taken hold of her heart. Long icy fingers gripped round and squeezed until she thought she'd cry out in pain. 'And Domenic?'

'Had been at the palazzo. Looking to do some grand thing or other. Great ones for plans, those two. Came back for lunch and found the place ablaze.'

Isabella felt sick.

'Everyone rallied round. Did what they could. Planes flew over with sea water to douse the flames, but it was all too late.' Lucetta pushed back a lock of grey hair. 'They'd have been dead from the smoke before Domenic even got there.'

'How did he get burned?'

She shook her head. 'He was like a madman. Wouldn't listen to anyone and far too strong to be held. He broke a window and went in.'

And who could blame him when the people he loved had been inside? Isabella wrapped her arms around her middle and hugged hard. She'd seen firsthand how indomitable the human spirit was, but how did anyone recover from an experience like that?

'He didn't even make it as far as the staircase.' Lucetta squeezed Isabella's cold hands, then turned and walked towards her kitchen.

Isabella followed, wondering what Lucetta thought her relationship with her stepson was. 'Did he have to be rescued?'

She nodded. 'He was in a coma for the first two days and then, when he came back to us, we had to tell him Jolanda and Felice had died.' Lucetta pulled open her large fridge and pulled out a glass jug of homemade lemonade. She set it down on the kitchen table, turning away to find some glasses.

Isabella rubbed her hands over her bare arms. She didn't want to hear any more. Not from Lucetta. She thought about the night before. The quiet and the peace of the sunrise and how he'd thanked her for letting him talk about Jolanda.

She reached up and brushed a tear away before it started. But Lucetta wasn't finished with her yet.

'Jolanda was a lovely girl,' she said, pouring lemonade into a glass. 'Shouldn't have really looked at a boy like Domenic. Not with her family's money. And until he met her Domenic was a little bit wild…'

She handed across a glass. 'It was her family that were the hoteliers, you know? Of course, Domenic has taken it all onto another level, but the start of it was Jolanda's grandfather. Bought his first hotel in nineteen thirty-seven. Held onto it through the war.'

'Did they blame Domenic for the fire?'

'No. No, not at all. It was no one's fault. But Domenic blames himself for her being on Mont Avellana even though that was very much her decision. She loved it here.'

Lucetta filled a second glass. 'The Palazzo Tavolara was going to be the start of something much larger on the island.

I don't know what she'd have made of this idea of building on Niroli. Not a lot, I suspect.'

Her words left Isabella feeling confused—on so many levels. She was trying to absorb too much information too quickly.

'Why?'

'Because her dream was for Mont Avellana,' Lucetta said, reaching for a tray.

Isabella stood with her hands clasped around her lemonade. 'Then why hasn't he developed the palazzo into a hotel?'

'He finds it difficult to be here. We all know that. But he can't quite bring himself to sell it either.' Lucetta placed a crocheted circle with small beads on it over the top of the lemonade and set the jug on the tray beside the empty glasses. 'The place is hanging like a millstone around his neck.' She picked up the tray. 'Would you mind taking Domenic out a glass of lemonade? The step down is difficult carrying a tray.'

Would she mind? Actually, yes. For reasons she couldn't even begin to understand she felt…nervous. It was almost as if she'd been given a small window into his soul and she wasn't quite sure what she wanted to do with that information yet.

So many questions—and no possibility of asking them.

Isabella picked up the glass and walked slowly back to the shady pergola. Back on Niroli it had seemed all so straightforward. The Vincini Group was the perfect match for…

And then she stopped.

The *Vincini* Group. Why was it called that if its origins lay with Jolanda's family? There was so much she didn't know about him.

And so much she wanted to know? Isabella shook her head. She felt as if cold water had suddenly started to run round her veins in place of blood.

She couldn't be falling in love with Domenic Vincini. That wasn't possible. *Was it?* There were hundreds of men who'd come to her at a click of her fingers and she was falling for a man whose heart was buried with his dead wife and child. A man whose scars were both inside and out. A man who sought solitude and a life away from the limelight.

Isabella stopped in the doorway.

'Is that for me?'

She swallowed. 'From Lucetta. She asked me to bring it out,' she said, moving nearer.

'Thank you.'

'You're welcome.' Most often, when she was talking to him, she wasn't aware of the scars at all. But now, having seen what he'd looked like before the fire…she was reminded.

'Is Carlo still asleep?'

'Yes.'

She looked at the ridged scars running the length of his face and wondered what had happened to him inside that burning house. Had glass exploded in his face? Had he fallen?

And what percentage of his body had been burnt? Looking at him now, all she could see was the puckered skin at the base of his neck. How far did it spread across his body? *Would it change the way she was starting to feel about him?*

Domenic laid his book to one side. 'What did she tell you?'

Her eyes flew guiltily back up to his face. 'What?'

'Lucetta. What did she tell you? And don't say "nothing",' he added with a tight smile as she started to reply.

Isabella sat down on the seat opposite, wondering what and how much to say.

'Did she talk to you about the fire?'

'Would you mind if she had?' Isabella asked cautiously.

His hand moved across his face and Isabella recognised she'd seen that mannerism many times. It was what he did when he was uncertain and thoughtful.

He shrugged nonchalantly, but his voice was bitter. 'I wish people didn't feel the need to but, I suppose, it's an unrealistic expectation.'

'She loves you.'

'I know that.' Domenic drained his lemonade in one go and placed the glass down on the table. 'It's why I come here.'

Isabella sipped her lemonade, feeling the ice cube knock against her teeth. This conversation felt a lot like stepping through a minefield, uncertain where to tread and what to probe, but there were things she needed to know. 'Is it true Jolanda wouldn't wish you to build on Niroli?'

'Why do you say that?'

'Is it?'

Domenic stood up restlessly and walked over to the edge of the pergola and looked out towards the granite mountain. 'Niroli wasn't an option when Jolanda was alive.'

'But if it had been?'

'Jolanda loved Mont Avellana,' he conceded, his hand moving across his face once more. 'She had a passion and a vision for this place. She loved the fact it was an island and a world unto itself. She loved the patchwork of local dialects, the different cultures and customs concentrated into such a small area.'

'Do you think she would have minded?'

Domenic turned to look at her. 'Yes.'

Yes. A simple, straightforward answer. Isabella placed her glass carefully down on the table, hugging her knees against her chest.

'Perhaps. Jolanda wanted to make Mont Avellana *the* tourist destination in the Mediterranean. It was her dream and she was passionate about it. It didn't matter to her that there's only the tiniest of airports and that the only way to drive across this island is via an inconvenient web of twisting local roads. I think she'd have been sad more than anything else.'

'So why haven't you done it? You could have developed the palazzo and—'

'I've had other projects.'

Isabella waited, watching as he moved to sit back down. The silence stretched out.

'It was never the best option for us, but Jolanda wasn't particularly interested in the financial payback. She'd been born to money and never thought about that side of things because it had always been there for her. What she wanted was to be part of something from the start. She wanted to put down roots in a place and really belong.'

'So…has not doing something with the palazzo been a financial decision or an emotional one?' Isabella prompted when he stopped.

'A little of both. I would find it hard to do it without her.' Domenic's mouth twisted. 'And things have undeniably changed since we bought the palazzo. Niroli wasn't the tourist destination it is now, for a start. If there's to be a magnet in this part of the world it won't be Mont Avellana.'

'But if you know she'd have hated you to be part of any development on Niroli, why am I here?'

'Honestly?'

She nodded.

He smiled. 'Because you said you wanted to create something that would rival the Costa Smeralda.'

Isabella frowned, not understanding.

'It could have been her speaking,' he said, softly. 'She wanted to create exactly that. And then you said you could do something for Mont Avellana and it seemed a good compromise.' He shrugged, picking up his book and shutting it.

She was here to salve his conscience by doing something for the island his late wife had loved so much.

'Is it enough?' Isabella looked across at him, struggling to find the words to ask what she wanted to know. She bit her lip. 'I don't want you to commit to Niroli if you feel you're betraying her memory. I know we had an agreement, but—'

'I've given you my word. The papers are already with my lawyers. When I'm back in Rome on Thursday, I'll sign.'

That should have made her feel euphoric—but it didn't. In her entire life, she'd never felt quite so muddled.

And she'd think more about why that was when he wasn't there to see it.

CHAPTER SEVEN

DOMENIC stood and watched Isabella's car drive down the heavily rutted track—her bodyguard beside her, motorcycle outriders forward and back and Silvana following behind in her own car.

And he wished that it had been him going with her. For the first time in four years he felt left behind.

This evening she would walk through the narrow cobbled alleyways and arches of Caprera. She would watch the sunset and eat *gelato*. Everyone would be charmed by her and he wouldn't be there to see it. He wouldn't share it with her. See her face. *Hold her hand.*

A shadow fell across him and his stepmother reached out a hand and tucked it into his arm. 'Come and have something more to eat.'

'No. No more.'

'Come anyway.' Her eyes were fixed on the short procession. 'Come,' she said, pulling on his arm, and they started walking back towards the stone villa. 'She's a good woman. Your father is impressed. Very impressed.'

Domenic looked down at Lucetta. 'With a Nirolian princess? Surely not?'

She shook her head. 'You shouldn't mock him. You know Alberto has only ever wanted what was best for Mont Avellana. And your Princess Isabella is certainly turning the world's eyes in our direction. Exactly as you knew she would when you asked her to come here…'

'And you don't like it?' he asked, picking up on something indefinable in her tone.

'It doesn't matter what I like.'

Domenic's smiled twisted. 'But that didn't stop you telling Isabella that Jolanda wouldn't have wanted me to build on Niroli.'

She gave a significant sniff.

'You shouldn't have done it. Isabella offered to release me from our agreement.'

'That would be the best thing for you. You shouldn't do business with her.' Lucetta stopped walking. 'I think she's a lovely woman doing a remarkable job…but she's not for you, Domenic.'

'Luc—'

'Don't.' His stepmother crossed her arms in front of her. 'Don't even think of lying to me. I can see the way you watch her and I'm worried for you.'

Domenic squinted up to the clear blue sky. 'I won't marry again.'

'That worries me, too. Jolanda wouldn't have wanted you to live like you do. She wouldn't want you lonely. No wife. No *children*.' Pain must have flicked over his face because she added quickly, 'I know I'm not supposed to say that to you. We all pretend…but, Domenic, Felice is in your heart until the day you die whether you have other children or not. And love stretches. If you have other children some day you will love them with all your heart, but you won't love Felice any less.

'I want to see you happy…but…Princess Isabella?' She shook her head sadly. 'No. She is not the wife for you.'

Domenic's hand moved against the ridged skin of his neck. 'You don't need to say this,' he said, more roughly than he'd intended.

'Think about her life. What it is like. Isabella Fierezza lives in a goldfish bowl. The only reason she could be here today without photographers straining to get her picture is because no one would have dreamt she'd be here.'

Because her itinerary stated she'd be at the Cattedrale di Caprera. He knew that. And her Chief of Security had been nervous in spite of it.

'That's not a life for you. Paparazzi chasing your picture when you even struggle to go to your father's party because of the way people stare.'

No, that wasn't a life for him.

'I want you to find a nice Mont Avellanan girl. Make a good home and stop pushing yourself to make more and more money that you don't want or need.'

Domenic pulled a hand through his hair. Lucetta saw too much, but how he felt about Isabella was an irrelevance. It changed nothing.

He had to believe that. On Thursday he would fly back to Rome and everything would go on as before.

'What Isabella is doing,' Domenic began quietly, 'she's doing because I want something for Jolanda. That's it. Niroli is business. Good business. And I'll run it at a distance like all the other hotel complexes we have around the Mediterranean.

'But…' His throat worked. 'Jolanda loved *this* island. I've not forgotten…and I saw a chance to do something in Mont Avellana. Maybe I can develop the palazzo into some kind of a hotel? Maybe a restaurant? I don't know yet. Something.

'But, I honestly believe Jolanda would have understood what I'm doing. Disappointed it wasn't what we planned…but understood. If I can't make her dream happen in its entirety at least I can give her something.'

This was about nothing else.

His feelings for Isabella were just that—feelings. And feelings could be conquered. *Damn it,* he was living, breathing proof of that.

Lucetta might hope he'd marry again. Might wish he'd have another child some day. Children. But that wasn't going to happen. It had taken years to find any kind of peace. It would take an incredible kind of courage to risk loving again and he wasn't that brave. Losing the people he'd lived for had broken him.

But, in all the suffering, he had learnt something about life. He knew how precious it was. How vital it was that you grabbed every day and lived it to its full potential. And he wanted that for Isabella. He wanted to see her happy.

Lucetta took hold of his arm. 'Just be careful, Domenic. Hmm?'

Home.

The thought slid into Isabella's mind the minute the palazzo came into sight. A place of refuge.

Strange she should feel like that about the Palazzo Tavolara when she'd never felt like that about the Palace in Niroli. Being in the fourteenth century fortress made her feel confined and…tired somehow.

She was tired now. Her face hurt from smiling and her feet ached from the beautiful Rodrigo Brambilla shoes. As soon as the high gates shut behind her she felt her body relax and a sense of peace pervade her soul.

It was getting harder and harder to play the part of Princess Isabella of Niroli. And that probably had a lot to do with Marco's decision to relinquish the crown. She glanced out of the window, watching the shadows. How could he have done this to her? Had he even thought what the consequences of his actions would be for her?

Isabella bit her lip as guilt slipped in. *Of course,* she hadn't been a factor in his decision. He'd given up the throne for the woman he loved. For Emily. She even thought he'd made the right choice.

But...

'Are you tired, Your Highness?'

Isabella turned her head to look at Tomasso. 'No more than you, I imagine.' She smiled, outwardly calm. 'At least I got to eat ice cream.'

Her companion smiled. 'I wouldn't swap.'

The car pulled smoothly to a stop and the door opened. Isabella twisted in her seat and climbed out with a practised flick of the legs.

'What would you like done with the flowers, Your Highness?'

Isabella turned her head to look at the beautiful bouquets she'd been presented with. 'Could you see if there's a local hospital or hospice nearby that would like them?'

'Certainly, ma'am.'

She skipped up the wide steps, hoping that Domenic would be there to meet her. She wanted to tell him about the man who'd bowed so low his toupee had slipped, and about the woman who'd been so shocked to see her that she'd walked straight into one of those twisting lampposts.

Silly things. Things she couldn't normally tell anyone…

But everywhere was quiet. Mia walked down the staircase towards her but her eyes were fixed on something behind. *Someone.* Isabella didn't turn round. She knew without looking. Tomasso. A gentle ache gripped her heart. Her Chief of Security had someone waiting for him. She had no one.

Where was Domenic? She wanted to see him.

'That all went well, I think, but I'll be glad to get out of these shoes,' she said with one foot on the stairs. 'Good night, Tomasso. And thank you.'

'Are the shoes particularly uncomfortable?' Mia followed her up to her room with its pale rose-coloured walls and eighteenth-century furniture upholstered in a rich plum.

'Very.' Isabella slipped them off and walked over to the elegant balcony and looked out. There was no glimmer of light anywhere. No indication that Domenic had stayed up in the hope of seeing her. No indication that he'd stayed up to enjoy the cool of the night either.

He was nowhere to be seen and she felt a rush of disappointment. She'd hoped to see him. Talk to him.

'We have a message for you, Your Highness,' Mia said from the depths of the room behind her. 'Signora Cattaneo is staying on Mont Avellana for a few days.'

Isabella turned back into the room. *Bianca.* Here?

'She's staying with her husband's parents.'

'That's fantastic.' It was more than fantastic. Isabella pulled the pins out of her hair and ran her fingers through the lacquered curls. 'Is Stefano with her?'

'She didn't say so, ma'am.'

Which probably meant he wasn't. Stefano would be unlikely to take time off at such short notice but, in a way, that made it better. She rarely had any time with her friend alone now. 'I'll contact her first thing. It's too late to do it now.'

As she spoke she looked out through the double doors. 'I'd like my white trousers and…oh, anything comfortable and cool. I really don't mind. I think I'll read on the balcony for a while.'

She wouldn't be able to sleep yet awhile. *Where was Domenic?*

'I've left an outfit on your bed, ma'am.'

'Thank you. Thank you very much.'

'Good night, ma'am.'

Isabella heard the click of the door and walked back into her bedroom, sliding down the zip of her pale green dress.

She couldn't quite believe it. Bianca was here on Mont Avellana. She might not have many friends she could trust implicitly—but those she had were very precious.

She pulled on the loose white cotton trousers and silk caftan top, before laying the pistachio wrap-over dress on the bed. Mia would have to do something clever about the creases if she was ever to wear it again. Though that was unlikely if any of today's photographs found their way into the world's papers.

Goodness, she was tired! Aching feet, aching face… Isabella stepped out on the balcony again, leaning on the balustrade. She couldn't go on living like this. Day after day, city after city, handshake after handshake.

She needed to make some decisions about what she wanted. Maybe she should have taken the opportunity to talk to her old school friend about Luca being removed from the succession when she'd been in Rome…but it had been too recent…and she'd felt too angry. With her grandfather, with Luca and with the situation as a whole. But this time she would.

Isabella lifted her hair off the back of her neck and felt the breeze cool her warm skin.

Isabella wandered aimlessly back out to the bedroom and over to the desk. The leather cover of her grandmother's diary was shiny from where she'd turned it over in her hands so many times. She picked it up and glanced back towards the balcony.

Where was he?

Domenic might have decided that he wouldn't spend another evening on the *terrazzo,* wouldn't watch another sunrise, but she…wanted to smell the mimosa, eucalyptus and oleander that hung in the air.

More than that, she wanted to take back some special memories of this place and lock them deep inside for the difficult times ahead. Because they were coming.

Queen Eva's slyly triumphant face when she'd learnt it would be one of her grandsons on the throne told her that. Her grandfather's second wife couldn't have been more delighted. And now it wouldn't even be Luca. It would be Nico…

The doors that led out to the *terrazzo* were open. Isabella padded across the warm stone, loving the feel of residual warmth against her feet. There was the sense of being insignificant against a vast sky and of being able to breathe.

Being at the Palazzo Tavolara had the feel of being in an oasis. She stepped out onto the lush lawn. A miracle in such an arid climate. She'd never seen it happening but a lawn like this would need watering daily. Why did Domenic keep ownership of something that must be a huge financial drain if he had no intention of turning it into a hotel?

The only answer must be that it had an emotional connection for him. Memories of his late wife must be bound up in this place.

Isabella walked through the archway towards the swimming pool. The grass was soft against her bare feet. Cool. The cotton of her trousers flapped against her legs and she listened for the sound of the cicadas still chirruping. She might not have the courage to slip into the water without her clothes, but she did have enough to dangle her feet in.

She wasn't sure what stopped her walking. A sound. Something. An inner feeling that she wasn't alone, maybe? But her feet slowed and she approached the final archway cautiously, and then stopped. Listening.

Nothing—but her heart was pounding as she started walking again. Through the arch…

Domenic.

Here.

In the moonlight she couldn't see much more than the outline of his body. A shadowy figure. But she knew it was him. Her stomach immediately did a compete roll-over. She pulled a hand through her curls and stepped out of the cover of the bushes.

He was swimming down the length of the pool and didn't see her. His arms moved smoothly through the water, scarcely making a ripple. Long, clean strokes.

And then he reached the end and did an underwater flip and powered his way back the other way. The same easy stroke, the same clean movement through the water. She went to stand at the end of the pool.

Domenic's hand touched the tiles at the end and he looked up. His face was shuttered. Not pleasure. Not anger. He was resigned.

To what?

To her interrupting his solitude or her seeing how scarred his body was? Curiosity surged through her. For Isabella everything stilled. There was just this moment in all of time. Just the two óf them in all the world.

Water glistened on his olive skin. His thick hair was slicked back off his face and the arm he held out the water looked strong and healthy. Unblemished.

With one easy movement he pulled himself out of the water and stood before her. He was…

Male.

That was the word that sprang into Isabella's mind. He was unbelievably male. Strong. Powerful. And intensely beautiful.

Water droplets hugged the dark hair on his chest and her eyes followed the narrow line that ran across a muscular stomach until it dipped behind his tight swimming shorts. She couldn't help but notice the firm bulge and her blood sang in her ears.

He wanted her.

In this moment, here and now, he wanted her. It gave her the confidence to look lower. There were scars on his legs. White, feathery lines that must have come from exploding glass. A complex web that burst across the darker colour of his skin.

She looked up and into his dark brown eyes. He was watching, looking for her reaction. Waiting.

Isabella moistened her lips with the tip of her tongue. 'I-I couldn't sleep.'

'We both seem to have a problem with that.' Domenic turned and picked up a large white towel resting on a sun lounger. He held it in his hands, not attempting to cover the puckered skin of his burn scars.

They were there, too. Cruelly disfiguring. Just touching his neck and spreading out across his shoulder and down his left arm. Then in one deliberate movement he swung the towel across his shoulder.

Isabella swallowed and then sat down on the edge of the pool. As though his being here changed nothing she rolled up her trouser legs and dangled her feet over the edge.

The water felt warm, baked by the sun, but still refreshing. Her nail varnish shone dusky pink through the ripples.

'You ought to go in,' Domenic said from somewhere behind. 'The water is lovely.'

Isabella didn't turn round. She could hear the rasp of the towel on his skin as he dried himself. 'I rarely swim.'

'Why?'

'I'm not particularly good at it. Somehow I never managed to learn how to breathe properly.' She moved her feet in the water.

'It's the same principle as out of it.' She could hear the smile in his voice and knew he'd relaxed. Whereas she…*she* was pulled as taut as a bow string.

'Not for me. I must hold my breath somehow and I end up with a stitch.' She pulled her feet out of the water and stood up. Acutely conscious of being here so late. Of him. Of having not brushed her hair or checked her make-up.

Domenic had put on a loose T-shirt and dragged on a pair of jeans, presumably over his wet swimming shorts. He held out his towel. 'Do you want this?'

'Thank you.' She took it and carried it over to a lounger, placing her diary on the small table beside it. The dark brown leather had one spot of water on it and she smoothed across it with her fingers.

'What's that?' he asked, sitting on the lounger next to hers.

'My grandmother's diary. Queen Sophia. My grandfather's first wife.'

Domenic nodded.

'Do you remember me telling you that she loved this place? My grandfather brought her here soon after they were married and they stayed throughout that first summer. Until she had to go back to Niroli to give birth to my father, actually—'

She broke off. She was gabbling. Stupid.

'I remember. She wrote about Poseidon's Grotto.'

'I thought it might be fun to read it here, so I brought it with me. I—' She stopped, mesmerised by the expression in his dark, dark eyes. More pupil than iris.

He did want her. She could feel it. Tension hung in the air like a tangible thing. It was real. Living. Vibrant.

And it scared her. It was like catching a wave and knowing you could do nothing but ride it out and see where it took you. Too powerful to be controlled, and that frightened her.

Never, ever, had she been out of control.

'May I?' Domenic held out his hand for the diary.

'Of course.' She brushed her hair out of her eyes. 'Y-yes, of course. It's quite hard to read. Her handwriting is very small and…'

Shut up! Just shut up!

Isabella held out the notebook and saw his hand move towards it. Long, beautiful fingers. Tanned skin. Tiny sun-bleached hairs standing up on his forearm.

And her fingers were millimetres from his. So close. One slip and they'd be touching.

Yesterday he'd held her hand, but this felt different. This wasn't about friendship. Or being lonely. It was about wanting and need. It was power and passion.

'How old was Queen Sophia when she came here?'

'Eighteen.'

'Young.' He opened the diary. 'When did she die?'

Isabella hugged her knees. 'Giving birth to my father. My grandfather was heartbroken. He really loved her. And she him.'

Domenic's dark eyes flicked up. 'I've not heard very much about her.'

'No, well…' Isabella picked up his towel and started to dry her feet. 'He married again and his new wife found it difficult. I think he took the easy path.'

'Does he speak about her at all?'

Isabella shook her head. 'No. But he gave me that. About eighteen months ago. Told me to keep it safe.'

The subtext being it wouldn't be safe in the hands of his second wife. That fitted with everything Domenic had heard about Queen Eva. By all accounts, she was a thoroughly dislikeable woman.

'And my father had a portrait of her. It hung in his dressing room. I think he liked to look at her, but didn't like anyone to see him do it.'

'Where's the portrait now?'

'Packed away waiting for Marco to decide what he wants to do with it.'

Primogeniture.

There was nothing fair about that. Domenic watched Isabella's hands twitch against his towel. She could never have expected to inherit. She wasn't the eldest child…but there was an edge to her voice that told him she was angry with her brother.

Whether that was due solely to his lack of action on their parents' possessions he couldn't tell. He only knew that every instinct in his body was prompting him to gather Isabella up and hold her close. Protect her. Shield her from whatever was troubling her.

She was inexpressibly lovely. Warm and kind. And he knew that each moment he spent with her meant he slipped just that little bit deeper in love. Millimetre by millimetre, centimetre by centimetre. She only had to turn her head and look at him to have every nerve ending in his body standing to attention. And when she smiled he responded with all the testosterone at his disposal.

It was a painful kind of pleasure. It would be so easy to ask if she'd like to see the grotto her grandmother had evidently loved so much. He'd be able to spend time with her alone but he knew it wasn't wise.

Here, within the perimeters of the Palazzo Tavolara, they were cocooned against reality. The real world wasn't so forgiving. Lucetta was right when she said there was no possible future for him and the Princess Isabella of Niroli.

He knew it. This idyll would end. It would end when he travelled back to Rome.

But it was so tempting to spend all the time he could with her. And Isabella would love Poseidon's Grotto. They could take a picnic…

Domenic shifted uncomfortably, his erect penis pushing against the rough denim of his jeans. He was being foolish.

But…

But when she'd looked at him, *really looked* at the discoloured and puckered skin on his shoulder, the scars that crisscrossed his body, there'd been no repulsion in her eyes.

None.

It had been the most intensely sexual moment of his entire

life. Her eyes had travelled down the length of his body. She'd seen every imperfection, must have seen his arousal…

And she'd not rejected him.

Seeing that had created an explosion in his head. She'd looked at him with curiosity. Even *desire?* Was that possible? Just the thought of her eyes on his body had the blood pumping through his veins, pounding in his eardrums.

It took every ounce of willpower he had to behave naturally around her. 'Did Marco inherit everything?'

Her eyes flashed up at him. For a moment he thought she'd not answer and then she relaxed again. She tucked her hair behind her ears and lifted her knees up to her chest. She looked younger than her twenty-eight years. Apprehensive. Rather as if she were staring out into a future and uncertain what it might hold. He wished he could help her. Really help her.

'Yes, of course. Everything that doesn't belong to the Crown. Marco inherited my father's personal effects. Rosa and I were given my mother's jewellery. Pieces that she'd brought into her marriage from her own family. Most of her jewellery belongs to my grandfather and will pass to his heir.'

Her fingers carefully untwisted the rolled up cotton of her trouser legs. Domenic watched the rhythmic movement, amazed by how uninterested he was in who would become King after King Giorgio's death.

Three weeks ago it had bothered him intensely. Rumours and counter rumours had started to come out of Niroli. Some of them so outrageous they defied belief…

She smoothed her hand down the fabric and wrapped it round her feet. 'I don't resent it,' she said, looking up. 'I inherited from my maternal grandfather. It's how I have money to invest in Mont Avellana. He was very generous to all of us.'

But that didn't make it any easier for her to see her mother's jewellery given elsewhere. That had to hurt. Domenic watched the muscle pulse in her cheek, the shadow of something in her eyes.

She might not resent Marco for inheriting the bulk of her parents' estate. As she said, she was independently wealthy. He'd checked it…

But…she *was* troubled. Perhaps angry with Marco for stepping aside from the succession? It would be ironic if he discovered, now he was morally committed to building on Niroli, that he'd been right to be concerned about who would be the next king.

Prince Luca seemed unlikely now. *Prince Nico?* What kind of man was he? Strange to think that Isabella, as the eldest granddaughter, would be the queen-in-waiting now if Niroli had adopted the Danish approach.

Setting aside his republican beliefs for a moment, he thought she'd have made an excellent queen. Every time she spoke about Niroli she lit up from the inside.

When had Nico Fierezza first left the island? Domenic tried to do a rapid calculation and failed. He'd no idea…but it had been years ago. Marco, too, had made his life elsewhere. But Isabella had stayed. And worked. And planned for her island home.

'Would you have wanted to be Queen?' he asked, watching her face. 'If your grandfather changed the rules of succession?'

'He won't.'

'But if he did?'

Isabella looked away. 'There's no point even thinking about it hypothetically. My grandfather believes there's strength in tradition…and he has an old-fashioned view of the role of women.' Her fingers plucked at her cotton trousers.

'But would you want it?'

Isabella hesitated and then answered quietly, 'Yes.'

'Does he know that?'

'Quite possibly but we've never talked about it. Nico will be the next crown prince.'

'Not Prince Luca?'

She shook her head. 'Not now. One scandal too many.' Her fingers continued to pluck at the fabric of her trousers. 'I think if Luca had been prepared to…*flatter* grandfather, for want of a better word, everything would have been fine.

'But Luca isn't that kind of man. He's too honest. He was never going to fawn about Grandfather like he wanted him to. At least, that's my take on it. It's all irrelevant now. Luca's in Queensland and barred from the succession. Did you know that?' she asked suddenly.

He nodded. 'Suspected it, anyway. I've been paying close attention to who will succeed King Giorgio. Prince Luca is to marry an Australian girl, I gather.'

'Megan,' she said, with a slight smile. 'Despite what you may have read about her, she's lovely. He'll be very happy, I think, and Nico will be the next king. At least, he's been summoned back to Niroli…'

'Will he come?'

Isabella tucked her hair behind her ears. 'Eventually.' She looked up. 'I think he'll take his time. He says he's got work commitments but it's more than that.'

Domenic watched the emotions flicker across her face.

She hugged her knees closer and rested her right foot on top of her left. 'Nico finds Niroli too confining. He's never going to be happy living back on the island. I can't see it. He's…fearless. I think that's the best word to describe him. I can't really explain him because I don't understand him. But Niroli is far too insular a place for him. And, of course, he loves his work—'

'He's brilliant,' Domenic cut in.

'He is—and he'd have to give that up because no ruler is allowed a separate profession.'

'Can he refuse?'

'He can.' Isabella chewed her lip. 'And in many ways Max would make the better king. At least he loves the island but…' She shook her head. 'Nico won't refuse. He's a little like you in that his sense of family is central to who he is. He'll come. And I'm sure he'll be a good king.'

Isabella's fingers pleated the soft cotton of her trousers, clearly troubled.

'What does that mean for you?'

She turned her head to look directly at him, shock showing in her beautiful eyes—as though no one had ever thought to ask her the question. Then she smiled at him and he slipped another millimetre towards loving her. 'I-I don't know. In the short term, perhaps, nothing. But everything will change eventually. For one thing, Nico will have to marry and his wife will assume my royal duties. All I'll have is my secular career.'

Isabella stroked one finger over the dusky pink nail varnish on her big toe. Domenic followed the movement with his eyes, content to listen, knowing there was more. Even her voice had the ability to curl his insides into a hard knot of wanting.

'That's why I came to see you. In Rome.' She glanced up. 'I thought…if I could get you to sign then there'd be a real reason to stay on Niroli. I've always thought bringing all the strands of our tourist ventures together was a good idea. It just became more important when Marco chose Emily over the Crown.'

Her hand moved to rub her arm, the silver threads in the silk of her kaftan shimmering in the moonlight. 'I think Marco made the right choice. I do. I really do. It's only…'

'His decision altered your life,' Domenic finished for her. Too many people, it seemed, were thoughtless in their treatment of her. Had anyone even noticed how she was feeling?

'Yes. Yes, it has.' She moistened her lips with the tip of her tongue. 'But that could be exciting.'

He could easily imagine her racking her brain to think of a way to secure his involvement in her project. He'd known when she'd sat in his conference room that it was important to her without guessing at the reason why.

He laid the diary back on the table. And her ideas for Mont Avellana had sprung from her grandmother's description of the island. An island she'd been frightened to come to…

But she was here. Searching for something that she could invest in, something that would give her life purpose. Domenic pulled his hand across his face, his fingers feeling the scar tissue.

Queen Sophia had loved Poseidon's Grotto. And he knew Isabella would, too.

But…

It touched so close to Jolanda's dream.

A muscle clenched in his cheek and his question came out as a bark. 'Would…you like to see your grandmother's grotto while you're here?'

'I asked Silvana about that. When I first arrived. She said she didn't think it would be possible.' Isabella hesitated. 'She said you've consistently refused all offers to turn it into a tourist attraction.'

And he'd refused to develop the palazzo. Domenic's mouth twisted into a wry smile. 'I'd like to show you. I think you'd love it.'

'I-I would. My grandmother describes it as being like a mystical kingdom.'

Her eyes were wide…and very beautiful. Domenic deliberately looked away. 'Has my sister left you much free time?'

'How long will it take?' Isabella asked. 'I have slithers of time each day, but all of Tuesday is free.'

'Because of my father's party?'

Isabella nodded. 'Silvana thinks there'll be lots to oversee on the day before. She's busy again on Wednesday, of course, but I'm being taken on a tour of the island…to get an overall feel of it, so that doesn't involve her anyway.'

'Tuesday, then?'

'Are you sure?'

'Of course. Would you mind going early? Before it gets too hot?'

'N-no, not at all. Whatever suits you best.'

'Perhaps eight?'

Isabella nodded.

'I'll wait for you on the *terrazzo*.'

Her hands bunched against the towel in her hands. 'Domenic…'

He looked across at her, watching the expressions work over her beautiful face.

'Silvana told me the grotto was one of Jolanda's favourite places—'

He stopped her. 'It was.' Jolanda had found the caves awe-inspiring. Strangely it didn't hurt remembering that. 'It's a magical place. It might even be what you're looking for. Though I meant what I said. I'm committed to the resort on Niroli regardless of what decisions you make.'

'Thank you.'

Isabella still seemed sad to him, the expression on her face wistful. 'Whatever happens with the succession, you will always be the granddaughter of a king,' he said softly. 'Nothing will ever take that away.'

She said nothing for a moment, resting her head back and looking up at the night sky. 'When my grandfather dies I'll be merely a cousin of the king. I won't have any specific royal duties. I didn't mind so much when it was Luca. Silly! It's exactly the same now it's going to be Nico,' she said, standing up and folding the damp towel in half. 'Where shall I put this?'

It was like shutters coming down on her confidences. As though she'd suddenly realised she'd said too much, been indiscreet.

Domenic swung his legs off the lounger and looked up at her. He could feel her sense of isolation—and no one knew more than him what a bleak place that was to inhabit. 'You can trust me not to repeat anything you say.'

Her hands stilled. 'I know that.' She spun round. 'I do know that. It's only I never…I never talk about my family. I-I hope you know I didn't mean that I don't like Nico, or that he won't be a good king when his time comes, it's just…I don't know him as well and…'

Domenic stood up and reached for her hand. Her fingers twitched inside his and he watched as she bit down on her lip to stop it trembling. Inside him something snapped. The way she was feeling about herself was wrong. He'd do anything he could to change that. She had to know that her value wasn't defined by her relationship to someone else. Isabella was worth more than that. So much more.

And he didn't have the words to tell her. His free hand moved to cup firmly around the back of her neck, drawing her closer. He heard her shocked intake of breath, saw the widening of her eyes, but the feel of her soft hair on the back of his hand was more potent than any drug.

He felt her swallow.

'I-I'm used to working with Luca. Because of the c-casinos and…'

She was so beautiful. *Luminous.* Domenic moved the pad of his thumb along her jawline…because he couldn't help it. Her skin was soft, smooth and unblemished. His thumb touched her lips, full, red and trembling. He hadn't felt like this in the longest time.

He wanted her beyond reason.

It was as though everything about her was filling his senses, stopping his brain from functioning normally. He only knew that he wanted her so badly he ached. He wanted to comfort her, hold her, *love* her.

Her lips were so close to his. So close. He could feel her breath on his face. Warm. Sweet. His nostrils were full of the scent of vanilla that hung about her hair.

And her eyes met his, looking up at him. Almost black. Her eyelashes heavy with the tears she hadn't cried.

'Domen—'

Her husky voice breathed his name and he responded. Helplessly. His world shrank to this moment as he bent his head to kiss her. Her lips were warm. Responsive.

It was like a bolt of electricity shooting through his body.

He wanted to bury himself within her. Feel her respond to him. Hear her call out his name.

Her hand twisted out from his and she rested her palm against his chest. Both his cupped her face, tilting her head back as his tongue slipped inside her mouth. Warm and moist. He needed to taste her, had to…

His hand moved round to the small of her back and he could feel the warmth of her skin through the fine silk of her top. *Dear God…* He hadn't held a woman, kissed a woman, since Jolanda. Not since the fire…

Reality screamed in his head. *What was he doing?* This was madness. She couldn't want this. Domenic pulled back with an abruptness that left Isabella reeling. He reached out and steadied her.

'I'm sorry.' He pulled a hand across his ravaged face, feeling the ridges beneath his finger. 'I shouldn't have done that.'

'W-why?'

He sensed the question rather than heard it. The man he'd used to be could have comforted her like that—but not now. Not him. A woman as beautiful as Isabella belonged with someone equally beautiful. She needed to be with a man who could take her to charity balls and fund-raising dinners. She needed to be able to walk barefoot on the beach without any thought of finding shade. She needed a man who could bring her laughter.

Children.

His mind was suddenly filled with the image of her holding Carlo. The gentle expression on her face as she'd looked at the sleeping baby. The way she'd stroked the top of his head and curved her fingers round his plump foot.

Isabella would want children. Perhaps most women wanted children at some point during their lives? Certainly Jolanda had. Domenic pulled a hand up to cover his eyes.

Like a montage, memories flooded through him. Jolanda holding Felice. Jolanda blowing kisses on the soles of Felice's feet. Jolanda asleep on the bed with Felice lying spread-eagled beside her.

Happy. Laughing. He could see Felice's round face lighting with joy when he walked through the door. The small white rabbit she'd slept with each night.

Until the fire.

Until the fire.

Domenic's hand balled into a fist. Everything he loved had been snatched away that day. Jolanda and Felice had died in a smoke-filled room but he might as well have died with them.

He didn't have the courage to risk loving again. If he carried on with this…*madness,* Isabella would destroy him.

'Your work with your charities will continue.' His voice seemed to grate as he forced out the words. 'And the resort will happen. It's up to you to see that it benefits Niroli's economy at large.'

Domenic consciously relaxed his hands. This was difficult. Everything about Isabella made him want to gather her up in his arms and kiss her until she couldn't do anything but respond to him. He wanted to feel her body against his, feel the weight of her breasts in his hands. Instead he was going to walk away. And he was going to do it now.

'And encourage our islands to work together,' she said, wrapping her arms in front of her.

'That, too.' He forced a smile. 'If you achieve any kind of harmony you'll have done more than any Nirolian royal has managed in two hundred and fifty years.'

'I will.' Her dark eyes looked cloudy. Confused.

Domenic glanced back towards the palazzo. 'It's late. I should go in. Good night, Your Highness.'

CHAPTER EIGHT

ISABELLA put on her sunglasses, as much to hide her eyes from Bianca as to shield them from the sun.

'What did Domenic do then?' Her friend reached out for the suntan spray and aimed it at her legs.

'Nothing. He left. He muttered something about all the things I could do to benefit Niroli and went inside.'

'*After* he kissed you.'

'Yes.'

'And you've not seen him all day?'

'No. Silvana and I went to see a bird sanctuary this morning but he wasn't at lunch and he's supposed to be out this evening.'

Bianca set the bottle down on the floor beside her sun lounger. She wrinkled her nose. 'Sounds to me like he was running away.'

It had sounded like that to Isabella, too. But *why?* Why run away from something that had felt so natural and right?

'And he called me "Your Highness". He hasn't done that since I first met him.' Isabella closed her eyes against the prickle of tears. She didn't even know why she was so upset. She'd known him for a mere handful of days. They'd shared one kiss...

One.

She didn't understand why it felt so precious. She only knew that when he'd walked inside she'd never known rejection like it. Or what it really meant to be alone.

Because it had been rejection. It had been in his eyes.

'Maybe he's got a problem with the royal thing,' Bianca said. Isabella could hear her settling back down on the lounger. 'You know, it would be amazing for a Vincini to be in a relationship with a Fierezza.'

'I know.'

'You're up against centuries of rivalry. Stefano said there were a fair few pokes at Domenic when he first starting doing business with Prince Luca, simply because of his close connection to King Giorgio. It wasn't well liked on Mont Avellana.

'And you know yourself how many concerns were raised on Niroli when you decided to approach the Vincini group. Old prejudices run deep. He must be aware of that. I don't know why it isn't bothering you more. *Hell,* just think what your grandfather would say!'

King Giorgio would quote the rule book at her. Recent events meant that she knew it verbatim. 'No marriage is permitted if the interests of the island become compromised through it.' She was on dangerous territory. She knew it. There was no point starting a relationship with a man who was forbidden to her.

Only…

Only she'd never felt like this before. She'd never met anyone who seemed to want to know her. They were all fascinated by the princess, when she wanted someone to love the woman.

Her grandfather probably wouldn't understand that either. Certainly not when the man in question was a Vincini.

Isabella turned her head and looked at her friend through her dark lenses. 'Then why did Domenic kiss me at all?'

Her friend laughed. 'Don't be silly. You're beautiful. He's a man.' Bianca lifted a hand up to shade her eyes from the sun. 'You must have had men kiss you before in the heat of the moment…?'

'Of course.'

But rarely. Most were in awe of her royal status—and those that ventured so close had never stopped so abruptly. Or so strangely.

Isabella frowned. It hadn't felt like a kiss in the 'heat of the moment' either. Certainly not one that should be regretted. It had come out of a feeling of closeness. A real *connection.*

She'd told him things she'd not confided to a living soul. Not even her sister knew she'd be glad to succeed their grandfather. She certainly hadn't even hinted to Rosa that, with Nico as the future king, she was scared of becoming obsolete and angry she'd been trained to fulfil a role that was no longer hers to occupy.

But Domenic had effortlessly understood. He even seemed to understand the knife edge she lived on—one half of her embracing her royal duties and the other feeling trapped by it. He'd seen past the carefully packaged image she presented to the world and found *her.*

And she knew him. Which was why she knew Domenic had pulled back for altogether more complicated reasons than her family background. There were probably many strands to it…and that was what scared her.

'Maybe he feels guilty about asking if you want to see the grotto? If his wife loved it there so much,' Bianca offered beside her. 'And, if he does, he'll certainly feel guilty about kissing you. Perhaps he still feels married in his head?

'You know I've not heard of him getting involved with

anyone since his wife died. And he must have had plenty of opportunity because he's so incredibly rich.'

Isabella pushed her sunglasses up on top of her head. 'Bianca!'

Her friend shrugged. 'It's life. Rich men are always targeted by women who like the things they have and are prepared to put up with them. But there's never even been a whisper of a rumour about him. I'm sure I'd have heard if there was. He seems to like to be alone.'

Domenic was fiercely alone. Inflexibly and determinedly. Only sometimes she seemed able to cross the divide. Isabella set her glasses back on her nose and lay back. Perhaps Bianca was right and Domenic felt guilty. The sun warmed her skin but didn't touch the cold knot that had settled inside her.

'He's probably got that thing survivors get sometimes,' Bianca continued. 'I read about that somewhere. Apparently people who've been through a sudden tragedy find it difficult to allow themselves to live normally. They almost think they should have died.'

Isabella immediately thought of the photograph Lucetta had shown her. Standing beside Jolanda, Domenic had looked like a very different man—and those differences were not entirely due to the physical scars. The changes in him went deeper.

'And, he *must* have body issues.' Bianca sat up abruptly and Isabella opened her eyes to see why. Her friend reached for her iced water and sipped. 'I don't know what proportion of his body was burnt in that fire but I'd heard he's had skin grafts and the like. Hell, I've got issues about the way my body looks after having Fabiano. I imagine burns scarring must be worse.'

Isabella closed her eyes again, safe behind the dark lenses.

Bianca's words conjured up the image of a scared and grieving widower, with an inbred distrust of her family—and she was right.

Only…when she was with Domenic it didn't feel like that. It felt a lot like coming home.

How did she make him feel?

Last night she'd been so conscious of her own reaction to the scars on his body she hadn't really thought about how difficult it must have been for him. In some deeply private place she'd been worried she might find the sight of them unattractive and she'd been flooded with relief when she hadn't.

Had she hurt him? Had he been uncomfortable? But then he'd gone on to offer to show her Poseidon's Grotto. Was he regretting that as much as the kiss?

'What are you going to do?'

Bianca's question forced her to open her eyes again. She wasn't sure what she was going to do. Truth be told, she wasn't even sure what she wanted. Everything was so confused in her head. All she really knew for certain was that when he'd pulled away from her it had felt as if something very precious was being taken away from her. And she wasn't ready for that to happen.

'Bel?' Bianca prompted.

'I don't know.' Isabella pushed her glasses back onto the top of her head. 'I suppose I'll see what he does next.'

'And if it's nothing?'

'Then it's not meant to be. I suppose that might even be for the best.'

She'd never stepped outside of what was expected for her as a Princess of Niroli—it seemed unrealistic to expect she'd do it now.

* * *

Isabella picked up her camera and thought about what lenses to include in her bag. Her grandmother had talked about the long walk down to the grotto so she didn't want to overburden herself with equipment.

On the other hand, there was nothing worse than seeing something and knowing it would make the most perfect shot and not having the right lens.

Always assuming she got there.

Isabella bit on her bottom lip. What would she do if Domenic wasn't there? Worse still, what would she do if he was there to tell her he'd changed his mind, that he thought it would be a mistake? That had to be a possibility.

She swung her bag over her shoulder and headed for the door with ten minutes to spare. She had to try and do what she'd told Bianca she would—she'd be guided by him.

Whatever his feelings for her, she *did* want to see the grotto. For as long as she remembered, she'd been told she bore an uncanny resemblance to her paternal grandmother and being given her diary had only fostered that feeling of connection. Staying at the Palazzo Tavolara, walking where she'd walked, was rather special.

She pushed the door open into the sitting room, her eyes immediately looking out towards the *terrazzo*. The doors were open, but there was no sign of Domenic. She pulled her bag up higher on her shoulder, feeling foolish.

Isabella glanced down at her wristwatch and then back at the empty *terrazzo*. It wasn't quite eight. There was still time.

'You're early,' Domenic said, coming up behind her. 'I'm sorry I've kept you waiting.'

And immediately she was covered with uncertainty.

She pulled on the strap of her bag and turned to look at him. It took a moment before her eyes adjusted to the comparative gloom inside. He looked casual and relaxed. Sexy. 'Are you happy for me to take pictures of the grotto?'

He moved closer and the jagged red lines on his face stood out starkly. 'As long as you don't include me in any of them. Are you ready to go?'

Isabella nodded. 'Are you sure you still want to do this today? I-I can always—'

'I want to,' he said, cutting her off. 'Is your security team happy for you to go alone, or do we need to wait for someone to join us?'

'No. I mean, we can go alone.' The words were out of her mouth before she felt a sudden wash of confusion. Perhaps he didn't want to be alone with her? Hadn't expected it? In twenty-eight years she couldn't remember *ever* having felt like this.

It was a mixture of excitement and paralysing fear.

'Only it is possible to get to the grotto by boat.'

'Do many people do it?'

Domenic shook his head. 'I own the mooring. But it's not as secure as it is closer to the palazzo. I'm happy to wait for a bodyguard to join us, if you'd feel safer.'

She didn't want that. For the first time she really understood why Luca evaded his protection. She wanted to be alone with Domenic. Just the two of them.

She moistened her lips. 'I'm sure it'll be all right. It's not a controversial place for me to be. Everyone knows I'm looking at potential tourist sites.'

He nodded and reached down to pick up a bag from the floor. 'What did you think of the bird sanctuary yesterday?'

'It was lovely,' she said, flicking her hair back off her shoulder.

Domenic's face changed. A far softer smile than she'd ever seen him give curved his mouth. 'I hate it, too.'

'I didn't say that.'

A wicked glint lit his dark eyes. 'But you thought it. And I agree.'

She choked on a laugh. No one ever saw through her like that. Everyone took what she said at face value. But not Domenic…

Not Domenic.

'We should think it's lovely.'

'I don't see why.'

'What they're doing there is important. It's only I don't know enough about it to make it interesting. That's my fault, not theirs.'

He glanced down at her and the expression on his face had her stomach feeling as if a million ants were let loose inside. And all at once she was glad she was here. Spending time with Domenic *was* a good idea. *It was.*

'I can't imagine Silvana enjoyed it much either. She's probably seen more of Mont Avellana in the last few days than in the rest of her life put together.'

'She does seem more suited to city life.'

'She is.'

It was on the tip of her tongue to ask which he preferred, but even that seemed a sensitive question. She already knew he'd lived on Mont Avellana until the fire had robbed him of his family. And that Jolanda had loved it here.

What she really wanted to know was whether he was still actively mourning his late wife. And how much of his reluctance to be with other people was because of his changed appearance and how much was because he was missing her.

Impossible questions.

They'd walked beyond anything Isabella recognised. Although it all seemed so familiar. Very like home. Everything about Mont Avellana was. The smells were the same, the flora and fauna…

'Please say if you want to stop to take any photographs,' Domenic said, following the line of her eyes as she was looking intently at some grasses. 'We've plenty of time.'

Isabella turned her head. 'I was just thinking this could be Niroli. I suppose I should have expected everything to be the same.'

'Disappointed?'

'No.' *Not at all.* She pulled at her camera strap. It was more that it made her sad that their islands had been so suspicious and resentful of each other.

Was that why he didn't act on the feelings she was sure he felt for her? Because she was sure he felt something. Sometimes when his eyes rested on her…

She tucked her hair behind her ears in a gesture she hadn't done since she'd left her teenage years. 'But I shan't take a picture unless it's something a little different.'

Jolanda's stunningly orchestrated gardens had long disappeared. Unerringly, as though he'd done it many times, Domenic led her along a narrow path through a pine forest until they emerged and Isabella could see the bright blue of the sea. As they walked closer to the cliffs the wild coastline took her breath away.

Instinctively she reached for her camera. 'Do you mind?'

'No. I don't mind.' He turned his face towards the sun and Isabella concentrated on finding the lens she wanted.

She squinted out across the sea towards a small island. 'Where's that?'

'Teulada. It's uninhabited.'

Isabella concentrated on getting her shot. Then she turned to look at him. 'There's a building on it.'

'That's a Spanish watchtower.'

'Spanish?'

'Niroli wasn't the only invader to come our way,' he said with a smile. He was doing that more often now. But...it was the kind of smile that held a hint of sadness, an underlying regret. 'It was built in the sixteenth century to protect against Arab raids.'

'It's beautiful,' she said, turning back to take another couple of shots. Strangely she was glad to be doing something familiar, something that always gave her comfort.

There was silence for a minute, but she knew his eyes were fixed on her profile rather than the distant island.

'How did you get interested in photography?'

Isabella put down her camera. 'I think it was probably a reaction to being photographed so much.'

He held his hand out to hold her bag while she released the lens from the camera. 'When I first started attracting attention I was very shy and found it difficult. My mother bought me my first camera. She thought it might help.'

'Did it?'

'Yes.' She smiled. 'Much to my surprise, it did. I started focussing more on what they needed from me to get a good shot.'

'Which explains why the world's press loves you.'

'I don't know about that. But I do try and make their job as easy as possible. If you don't it can be very painful.'

She knew Domenic thought about that, but she was grateful he didn't ask her to elaborate. If he was curious it would be easy enough to find the photographs she wished had never been taken.

He wouldn't though. He wasn't that type of man.

'Your pictures of Mont Avellana were stunning,' he said into the silence that stretched between them. 'I don't think I told you.'

It felt good to be praised by Domenic.

'Thank you.' She tucked the lens into its felt lined box and tucked it away in her bag. 'I'm getting better all the time. Some of my pictures are being used in Niroli's advertising campaign.'

'I didn't know that.'

'My favourite is the one of the amphitheatre.' She smiled up at him. 'But then, I like everything about that place. It has a real sense of history and I love to feel I'm connected to the past.'

Her foot stumbled on a rock and Domenic's hand shot out to steady her. It was warm against her skin and her breath caught in her throat. She was so attracted to this man. On every level there was.

'Careful. The path does get a little treacherous.'

Isabella's eyes searched his for a similar kind of awareness. It was there. She was sure of it. A telltale muscle pulsed in the side of his cheek and his smile was almost frozen in place.

'We can't rival your amphitheatre,' he said, his hand dropping back by his side. 'But you ought to get Silvana to take you to the ancient city of Chia.'

'What's there?' she asked, her voice breathless.

'Until nineteen seventy-five, people thought nothing. The records showed Chia as the capital of the Roman province of Mont Avellana but it was abandoned when they left and, over the centuries, was completely covered by sand.'

Domenic turned away. 'It needs some serious investment,' he continued, 'which our government have not given to it, but it's a fascinating place. So far scholars have identified the temple and the Roman baths but the site is far more extensive than that. And the mosaic-tiled floors are very exciting.'

'I-I'd be interested in that.'

'Tell Silvana. In fact, I will. I'd like you to see it while you're here.'

Isabella walked in silence. Some part of her must have been hoping that he'd offer to take her himself because she felt hurt—and that was foolish. Domenic was flying back to Rome on Thursday.

She had so little time with him. So little time to discover what it was that was drawing her to him. She brushed a stray hair off her face and took a shaky breath. 'Shall I send you my photographs when I get back to Niroli? Perhaps you could use them. Or give them to someone who could?'

He glanced across at her, his brown eyes warm. Isabella rushed into speech. 'Yesterday I managed to get some beautiful ones of the flamingoes on the salt flats. And the marshland had egrets and purple heron. I don't think they're so special. The light was fading by then, but I'll know better when I get home and look at them properly.'

He smiled. 'You really are passionate about photography, aren't you?'

'It's one of the few things I take seriously. I think about it all the time. It's become something of an addiction—'

Isabella broke off as she took in the steep steps carved into the limestone cliff. They stretched on and down towards a small cove. So beautiful.

Mutely, Domenic held out his hands to hold her bag. 'There are five hundred and seventy-three steps down.'

'You've counted?'

'Jolanda did.'

Isabella looked up, scared to ask the question and frightened to hear his answer. 'Does it hurt you to be here without her?'

'I thought it would, but, no. No, it doesn't.'

She knelt down to rest the lens case on the ground. 'I'm glad.' She was more than glad.

'How did Queen Sophia describe it in her diary?'

Isabella stood up again and trained her camera on the cliff face, bringing the steps into sharp focus. 'She says they took so long climbing back up they were late for dinner. I didn't imagine anything like this though.'

'It's quite impressive.'

Everything was impressive. Isabella had to concentrate on the steps as she walked down them. So many were uneven and there were places where it would have been easy to fall.

Domenic stopped in front of her and pointed. 'Look over there.'

Her hand automatically reached out to steady herself and she touched his back. It felt as if every hair on her arm stood to attention. Her fingers splayed out and she looked at the whiteness of her hand against the oatmeal colour of his linen shirt.

What was happening to her? She'd never been like this about a man. Not even the Rt Hon Justin Leagrove-Dyer had made her feel so reckless—and yet she'd been so infatuated with him. For a time. Until she'd discovered he'd been interested in her money more than her.

Slowly she removed her hand and looked where Domenic was pointing. Just appearing from behind a jut of rock was a long stretch of white beach strewn with juniper plants. High sand dunes gave way to the dramatic cliffs behind.

She immediately went for her camera and Domenic

laughed. It was the first time she'd heard him do that. Rich and warm. She looked up into his face and her breath froze.

His smile faded and his eyes flicked to her mouth and back to her eyes. *He was going to kiss her again.* She knew it. She didn't dare breathe and every thought she had was concentrated on willing him to do it.

Kiss me. Kiss me. Please kiss me.

His hands seemed to reach out for her, resting on her shoulders. Slowly, very slowly, he moved closer, his mouth touching hers.

It was exactly like last time. But the response his kiss provoked was like nothing she'd ever experienced before. It was gentle and demanding at the same time. Comforting and exciting.

Her hand fisted in the linen of his shirt. Her head was full of his name. Over and over.

Then she felt him pull away and heard the small groan she gave from the base of her throat. His thumb brushed against her bottom lip and he eased back further.

'Isabella…'

She opened her eyes.

'*Oh, God.*' His mouth swooped down on hers. His tongue flicking between her lips. Demanding. Seducing.

It wouldn't have mattered if she'd known a telephoto lens was trained on her. She wanted this so badly. It seemed Domenic's kiss was everything she'd been waiting for. Like the fictional sleeping princess, she felt alive because of it. Alive as she'd never felt before.

Moments later it was over. Domenic had pulled back again and Isabella was left feeling exposed and shaken. She reached out to take hold of his hand, his fingers instinctively interlocking with hers.

His hand was darkly tanned against the pale skin of hers. *His beautiful, beautiful hands.* So sexy.

'I can't seem to help but kiss you,' he said quietly.

Isabella struggled to find her voice. 'Is that a problem?'

The expression in his eyes made her want to reach for him. 'I think so.'

'Why?'

His eyes flicked to her mouth and her stomach clenched in response.

'Because it can't lead anywhere.'

'But why?'

He shook his head and then said quietly, 'We can talk about it later. Not now. I don't want to talk now.'

And neither did she. She didn't want to discuss what her grandfather's reaction would be to discovering she'd begun a relationship with Domenic Vincini. She didn't want to talk about Jolanda…

Domenic kept hold of her hand and led her down the final run of steps. His fingers felt so good against hers. Jolanda was dead…but she was *alive.* He had to see that.

And she needed him. Really needed him. The knowledge burst in her head like a sudden crack of lightning.

And he needed her.

Isabella held her breath as they approached the mouth of the cave. Her expectations were high but she hadn't even begun to appreciate the beauty of what she would see once inside.

She looked up at Domenic and found he was watching her, looking to see her reaction. Despite everything she smiled. 'This is unbelievably beautiful.'

'Come with me.'

They took the narrow path that led along the side of the natural lake. Rudimentary lighting had been placed in crevices along the wall. Presumably a remnant of Jolanda's plans for the grotto.

Isabella pushed the thought of Domenic's late wife aside. As long as he was choosing to hold her hand she was happy.

More than happy. Even her inability to take a photograph of what she was seeing failed to spoil the experience. Without additional lighting she'd never begin to capture the eerie beauty of the stalagmites.

It was like stepping into Tolkien's Middle Earth. Extra-ordinary and perfectly beautiful. No artist could have carved anything as beautiful. And around it all there was dark, still water.

'This is the second largest freshwater lake in the world,' Domenic said, his voice rumbling. The grip on her hand tight-ened. 'The tide can only reach so far. Certainly not enough to salt the underground water.'

Isabella felt a little as if she were walking in a church. She felt the same sense of awe.

'Through here is the largest of the chambers.'

A cavernous space opened up before her, more breath-taking than anything that had gone before. 'It's incredible,' she whispered.

'Yes, it is. When you think about it there had to be a reason why your ancestors went to the trouble of building the steps down here.'

'Did they?'

He nodded. 'They're as old as the palazzo.'

'I'm not surprised my grandmother loved it so much. She

planned on organising an orchestral concert here.' Isabella looked round and searched out the large flat area Queen Sophia had described. 'There I imagine.'

Domenic's fingers moved against hers. 'That would be beautiful.'

Her head was suddenly teeming with ideas. She could see the grotto lit with lanterns. Maybe even sculptures set into the alcoves and reflected in the dark water.

If Domenic was prepared to let her do it.

She shivered.

'Let's go and have some lunch before we attempt the climb back up. I brought something down with me.'

Isabella said nothing. Her time with Domenic wasn't over yet, but she could sense she was on borrowed time. He led her back out from the grotto and they stood for a moment blinking in the bright sunlight.

The heat was steadily climbing. She looked across at him, searching for signs of discomfort. Maybe the stiff breeze off the sea compensated.

Domenic released her hand and shrugged his small rucksack off his right shoulder. Isabella sat down and pulled out her camera, fitting the telephoto lens to it before turning back to look at the entrance to the grotto.

And, then, she took a picture of Domenic. Forbidden...but irresistible.

If he noticed he didn't say anything. His concentration was entirely on the picnic he'd brought with him. 'The focaccia is stuffed with sausage, ricotta, chard and red peppers.' He set it on a stone and added prosciutto, olives, tomatoes, fresh mozzarella and a large bottle of water. 'Are you thirsty?'

Isabella nodded.

He reached inside his bag and pulled out two plastic tumblers. His fingers brushed against hers as he handed it across. 'Not exactly fit for a princess,' he said with a tight smile.

'That would depend on the princess.'

He looked up from pouring the water. He'd understood exactly what she was trying to tell him. She watched him swallow and every fibre of her being wanted him to throw the bottle aside and kiss her again. Kiss her…and never stop kissing her.

'Have you thought about what King Giorgio would think? What he might do?'

Unbelievably it didn't matter. Didn't matter at all.

'It can't happen, Isabella. *We* can't happen.'

Her throat felt dry and it was suddenly difficult to swallow. She didn't know how to handle this situation. She wasn't even sure what she was fighting because he hadn't told her. He broke the focaccia apart and handed her a section of it.

'I'm not needed on Niroli now,' she said, painfully. Did she dare suggest she might even like to live in Rome? What would he say if she did?

'But you're still a Fierezza.'

She would always be that.

Domenic settled himself on the sand and looked out towards the craggy island with its oversized watchtower. 'We'd started to build there. Jolanda and I.'

Isabella forced down the piece of bread that had stuck in her throat.

'The idea was to make a holiday island. Very exclusive. Individual villas, each with access to their own private beach.'

'How far did you get?' Isabella managed to ask.

'Just one villa. The plans were all in place but then there was the fire and everything was shelved.'

The fire.

Isabella pulled her knees up to her chest and hugged them to her. Was he trying to explain why he didn't want to be with her?

'You ought to carry on with it.'

There was a pause and then, 'I think so. And, maybe, the palazzo, too.' He turned his head to look at her. 'What would you do with it if it were yours?'

'I'd live in it. Part of it, anyway.'

'On Mont Avellana?'

'If it were mine,' she said, watching the gentle lap of the water. 'And I'd build a restaurant in the grounds with views of the sea.'

But it wasn't hers. And soon, very soon, she'd leave Mont Avellana and she'd never return. 'Would it be different if I wasn't a Fierezza?' she asked on a burst.

Domenic turned slowly. 'You are.' He pulled a hand across his face. 'My father invited you to his party, didn't he?'

She nodded.

'And you've decided not to come.'

It was a statement not a question. Isabella's eyes didn't leave his face.

'Haven't you?'

'Yes.' Part of her had wanted to go; only Tomasso had expressed grave reservations. And, of course, she knew what the repercussions would be when she got home.

'I should never have kissed you.'

Words of protest formed in her head but they didn't make it out of her mouth.

'And you know I'm right,' he said quietly.

CHAPTER NINE

ISABELLA had had ample time to make her decision. Sitting on the balcony, long into the evening, looking out across the formal gardens. Then this morning over a solitary breakfast of persimmons and prickly pears…

She needed to go to Alberto Vincini's birthday celebration—and, though she was frightened, she would go.

Over the years it had apparently developed into a major social event, and drew both personal and political friends from all over Mont Avellana. She was completely aware of how big a statement she'd be making as far as the world's press was concerned.

It would be a grand gesture.

Tomasso had warned her that republican activists might use the occasion to draw attention to their political goals. And she knew what her grandfather would think when he saw the inevitable photographs.

But against that was the way she felt about Domenic Vincini. He'd made a unilateral decision about their future and she wanted him to see how little she cared about the politics of their respective families.

She also wanted to catch him off guard. Make him act without thinking.

Isabella deliberately chose a simple gold droplet to wear in her ears, rather than a flashier diamond.

'Would you like the matching necklace, Your Highness?' Mia asked twisting the final strand of hair up into a complicated twist of curls.

'Not if I'm wearing the flowers,' Isabella answered, watching as Mia placed three red roses in the honey-gold curls. The deepest shade of the petals picked out the exact colour of her long shift dress.

That, too, had been chosen for its simplicity. It was deceptive, though. Its high price tag was warranted by the clever cut, which meant the silk hugged her curves and dipped low on her back.

There was a firm rap on the door and Isabella turned her head.

'The car will be brought up to the front of the palazzo in ten minutes,' Tomasso said from the door.

Isabella nodded and gave her reflection a final look. 'Thank you.' She smiled up at Mia. 'Thank you, too.' Then she stood up and smoothed out the silk of her dress. It fell in soft folds around her ankles. 'I'll be down in a moment.'

She walked over to the balcony and looked out across the gardens as the door clicked shut behind her. *Jolanda's garden.* Was Domenic's love for his late wife another barrier? *The main one?* She didn't *know.* At the back of her mind she did wonder whether she was about to incur her grandfather's wrath for nothing.

Isabella turned abruptly and walked out of the room. It didn't help to think like that. Tomorrow Domenic was flying back to Rome. *Tomorrow.* There was very little time left.

Tomasso met her at the bottom of the dramatically beautiful porphyry stairs and led her out towards the car. Isabella gave him a brief smile and slid into the back seat, while he walked round to the other side.

'Ready?' he said, sitting beside her.

She nodded.

'Not surprisingly there's already considerable press interest in your going to the Vincini party. Do you still wish to use the main entrance?'

Isabella straightened her spine. 'It's not a secret I'm going, so let's not make it difficult for them to get their photographs.'

Then she looked back at the palazzo. It would be so easy to turn back now. She could plead a headache, even send a message that she'd decided it would be unwise…

The car surged forward and Isabella switched into professional mode. If nothing else she would at least have made the biggest gesture possible to heal the rift between Niroli and Mont Avellana.

But she was hoping for more. So much more.

They passed through familiar-seeming countryside. Along tiny roads with sweeping views of vineyards and wheat fields. And on through a city of wide tree-lined roads and imposing eighteenth century houses. Then they took the main road and headed out towards the coast.

Tomasso sat impassively by her, but she wondered what he was thinking.

'The villa is immediately round this bend, Your Highness.'

Isabella didn't need the warning. She could see the lights hung throughout the garden. Her car slowed and she heard the shout as the gathered photographers realised she'd finally arrived.

Fear gripped her. And excitement. That, too. It was a heady potion. For the first time in her life she really felt as if she was taking control of her destiny and finally stepping out from beneath the shadow of her family.

'Here we go.' Tomasso opened his door and walked round to open hers.

Isabella allowed herself one deep, steadying breath and then she smiled. She flicked her legs and stood gracefully, not needing the hand Tomasso offered her. Her performance was faultless. No one would have been able to guess how hard her heart was slamming against her rib cage.

'Your Highness, does King Giorgio know you are here?' one voice shouted louder than the rest. Mostly she could only hear her name above the general hubbub. 'Isabella.'

She paused as the cameras flashed.

'Princess Isabella!'

'Are you aware Alberto Vincini actively fought for independence from Niroli, Your Highness?'

Isabella turned to look at the woman whose voice was more insistent, her questions specific. It was a face she recognised, one of the pack that followed her everywhere.

'Giovanna,' she said, pulling the reporter's name from the recesses of her memory. 'In the years you and I have travelled together, we've seen the consequences of all kinds of violent conflict. I think anything that promotes understanding and peace is something that should be grasped, don't you?'

'And King Giorgio?' the steely-haired reporter persisted.

'Is keen for there to be good relations with Mont Avellana.' That, at least, was true. The fact that he'd prefer them to be on his terms was something that didn't need to be said here.

Silvana came into the small summer sitting room and shut the door. She perched on the arm of one of the chairs, slipping off her shoe to rub at her foot. 'Isabella's doing amazingly. I've seen her in action over the past few days, but what she's doing tonight is phenomenal.'

Domenic looked up from his book. 'I don't know why you're surprised.'

'And that from the man who said her chief skill was filling a designer dress to perfection…if I remember rightly!'

Domenic said nothing, merely running his hand down his face. Before he'd met Isabella he'd certainly undervalued what she did and how much she contributed. This time, though, he feared she had a different agenda.

'Dad's incredibly pleased she's come. He's taken it as a personal compliment.'

'It is.'

'Is it?' Silvana's right eyebrow rose a fraction. 'I'd have thought the compliment should go elsewhere.'

Domenic knew his sister glanced across at him but he kept his eyes firmly on his book. Silvana wanted him to have the fairy tale but the real world wasn't so kind. A twenty-first-century version of *Beauty and the Beast* would have a very different ending.

'Dad's introduced her to practically everyone,' Silvana said, slipping her foot back into her sandal and walking over to a side table. 'She must have shaken so many hands this evening she's in danger of getting repetitive strain injury.' She poured out a couple of glasses of wine and handed him the slightly fuller one, then sat down. 'How long are you going to stay in here?'

'I always keep a low profile at these things.'

'Not like this.'

Domenic felt a spark of pain in his right temple. He raised

a hand and moved it in concentric circles, hoping it would ease. It was difficult enough knowing Isabella was here, walking about the gardens, talking to his father's friends, without Silvana's version of the Spanish Inquisition.

Particularly when he wanted to be with her.

'You ought to be out there making sure Isabella's okay—'

'You do it.' He closed his eyes at the brusqueness in his voice.

'No. She's put herself on the line for you. I'm not a fool. I have seen the way you look at each other.'

'You don't understand—'

'I understand perfectly.' She stood up. 'So *what* if someone asks you how you got burned? This is self-indulgent, Dom. The truth is you're too bloody scared to get on with living and out there is someone more amazing than you deserve!' She walked across to the door, shutting it with a decisive click.

Domenic was left in semi darkness, just the light from a single lamp. He rubbed his hand across his face. Then he shut his book and stood up to pace restlessly towards the French windows. He looked out and listened to the soft music and the laughter.

Even with Jolanda he hadn't felt like this. He'd never experienced this…uncontrolled attraction he felt for Isabella. He'd not known what it was to physically desire someone so much that it consumed him.

But being with her was impossible. It was a line he couldn't cross—for very many reasons.

But wasn't the problem that he'd already crossed it? He was already in love with Isabella. He'd fought against using the word 'love', but he knew it was the only one that would do justice to the intensity of what he was feeling.

And he was running scared. A woman like Princess

Isabella of Niroli didn't belong with a man like him. And she'd realise that eventually. One day she'd leave him and he knew he wouldn't survive a second loss.

She was lonely. Certainly confused over her future. Maybe she even felt a misplaced sense of pity for him? He raised a hand to rub his temple. He couldn't bear that. Not *pity*.

The door opened suddenly and he turned expecting to see Silvana again. Instead he saw Isabella. His book fell to the floor and he stared at her.

She looked…like…

He swallowed. She looked too beautiful to rightly belong in this world. Domenic couldn't put words on it. Her beauty lit her from within. It was so much more than the dark red column of her dress and the twisting curls piled on her head. More even than the curves of her body or the fullness of her lips.

And he knew, with complete certainty, that whatever she did, wherever she went, he would love her until he died. It was like suddenly stepping into a beam of light.

He loved everything about her. The way she looked. The way she moved. The way she spoke. The way she thought…

He loved her. Simple as that. And it was a love that would rip him apart.

Isabella let go of the handle and quietly shut the door behind her. 'Silvana said I would find you here. Sh-she said this was the perfect place for sanctuary.'

'Do you need it?'

She smiled and her eyes sought his. He could read the plea in them. His hands balled by his side.

'A little. My face is beginning to ache from smiling.'

'Are people being friendly?'

'Very.' Her fingers strayed up to one of the gold teardrops

hanging from her ears. 'But there's dancing and saying no is becoming harder.'

Domenic reached down to pick his book off the floor.

'Do you have to say no?'

The deep red silk of her skirt seemed to shimmer in the subdued lighting as she walked. 'It's not obligatory, just wiser. And there's no one out there I wish to dance with.'

Her eyes were wide and soft like velvet. Domenic turned away to pick up the book and carefully placed it back on Silvana's colour-coded shelves. His mind was full of images of what it would be like to dance with her. How wonderful it would feel to have her body pushed up against his.

She glided over to one of his sister's most uncomfortable chairs and sat down. She reminded him of how he'd first seen her in his Rome offices—tightly controlled, a little nervous… and impossibly beautiful. Everything in him was straining to go to her. To let his hand cup her face and to tell her that everything was all right, that he loved her and wanted them to be together.

But that wasn't possible. It would never be possible. If she looked at him clearly she would see that.

'Have you been in here all evening?'

He steeled himself to tell her the truth. 'I came in when I heard you arrive.'

He knew he'd hurt her…but he'd intended to. She needed to see for herself how futile their attraction was. He wanted her to be the one to pull away because it would make it easier for him to accept it *was* futile.

But it was painful to see the fleeting expression in her eyes. 'Isabella…' He said her name on a groan. That single word was full of yearning, of everything he wasn't prepared to tell her.

'Please come out and join the party. Dance with me.'

'That's not possible. There are too many people with mobile phones who wouldn't be able to resist taking a photograph.'

Her fingers moved to twist the gold droplet again. 'We could just talk.'

Everything was warring inside him. What he wanted, what he thought was right for her. Guilt. Fear.

Mostly fear.

'And everyone would stare and whisper behind their hands.'

He turned his back to her. Silvana had placed lights artistically across her garden and huge lanterns with large creamy candles in them surrounded the pool. Romantically beautiful, particularly when it was combined with the music from Mont Avellana's premier orchestra.

And, more than anything in his entire life, he wanted to walk there with her. He wanted to hold her hand and for everyone to know she was his. *His.*

'They're doing that anyway. But everyone seems to like my dress, so it could be worse.'

Her dress was stunning. *She* was stunning. But she wasn't the woman for him. Lucetta was right. Isabella's lifestyle was one he couldn't embrace. Domenic's hand reached out for support and he rested it against the window frame. A light breeze tugged at his hair and he could feel it brush against his face.

'You might come and share the load.' He heard her stand up, move towards him. Her voice was low and hesitant. 'People will talk. You can't stop them.' There was a long silence. 'Please don't hide yourself away.'

'I'm not hiding.'

'Domenic—'

His control snapped. 'Go out and enjoy the party if you

want to, but leave me here. I'm tired of watching people's eyes try hard not to wander down to my neck.' He turned round. 'I hate seeing the shock and repulsion. What do you think they'd say if they thought ours was anything other than a business relationship?'

Isabella kept walking towards him. He could hear the soft rustle of her skirt and smell the faint scent of her perfume.

She stopped centimetres from him. Her eyes were half challenge, half fear. Then she lifted her right hand and gently stroked it down his face. Her forefinger traced the long scar from his eyebrow to his nose. Then she meticulously traced the second, which ran from the centre of his cheek to his jawline.

His body jerked in response. Then she stepped closer still. He could feel her breath stroking his skin. Her fingers moved against the burns scarring on his neck. The discoloured and puckered skin he hated to touch himself because he remembered the pain…and how much he had lost.

'I don't care what they say. I wish this hadn't happened to you,' she said, her voice husky. 'But you got these scars because you loved your wife and daughter enough to risk your life.'

Her voice was barely more than a whisper. And she was so close he could see each individual eyelash. They swept down across her pale cheeks and then she looked up into his eyes.

'There's nothing unattractive about that.'

Inside he was screaming.

'I need you.'

It was like a siren's call, impossible to resist. He could feel his body warming, every male instinct responding.

He knew how it felt to hold her. And he knew what it felt

like to push his tongue past her lips and into the softness of her mouth. He knew what she tasted like.

He knew how her body moulded itself against his. And he knew how her back curved and the warmth of her skin felt beneath his fingers. He *knew*.

'Dance with me.'

It wasn't a request. More a dare. Isabella waited for him to respond.

Suddenly his mind was flooded with an understanding of how Adam had been unable to resist Eve's offer of the fruit of the tree of knowledge. He knew his survival depended on his turning away…but he couldn't.

Didn't.

His hands reached for her and she seemed to be in his arms before he realised how it had happened. He pulled her closer. And closer. Every line of her body was pressed up against his. He didn't even care that the hard length of him was pushed up against the softness of her belly.

And then there was the music. Scarcely remembered Mont Avellanan pieces he couldn't have put a name to if he'd tried but they filled his senses. Her body moved against his and he felt his final resolve buckle.

His hand slid around her waist and he let his fingers feel for the bare skin of her back. He wanted that. He wanted to slide his hand around and cradle the weight of her breasts. Instead he let it slide down over her buttocks, pulling her in hard against his arousal.

'Isabella.' His voice was husky and broken. He had no resolve left. He wanted her. Needed her as much as it seemed she needed him.

And then she kissed him. An echo of what she'd done

before when she'd kissed his cheek. But this time she kissed his neck. Her lips were moist and warm against the part of his body he despised the most.

He hadn't allowed himself to cry since his mother died, but he could have cried now. Certainly lifted his head and howled at the moon.

Sexier than anything that had gone before. Isabella Fierezza was here to claim him. Deliberately she'd stepped over the line…

It would have been so easy to give himself over to the sensations of the moment.

But this was the most photographed woman in Europe. He couldn't do it. Her life was played out on too big a stage. And in the full glare of publicity.

She would want a life he couldn't give her.

Her hair smelt sweet and brushed against his cheek and he allowed himself to bury his face in it. He wanted to remember. His whole body responded to her scent and he felt her breath catch.

'Isabella.' *Oh, God. Isabella.* He wanted everything to be different.

She raised eyes that tempted. Her breath brushed across his lips. She was so close. Very close. If he dipped his head he could kiss her again.

Warmth seeped into the hand resting low on her spine and sensations flowed down the one holding her hand. He'd not danced for years but it seemed it was something one didn't forget. Domenic's hand tightened its grip on hers.

Isabella looked up and smiled and the last fingernail he had on restraint crumbled. He loved her and he was powerless to resist her. The truth of that flowed through him as though it were part of the almost Middle-Eastern-sounding folk music they were moving to.

Tomorrow he *would* leave. He would suffer every time he saw her picture, every time he read her name…

But tonight he would hold her.

She curved into him as though she'd been designed to fit there. Her hair brushed softly against his cheek. And she smelt as he imagined heaven would.

Then she raised her face towards his. Her eyes rested on his lips but she didn't move any closer. Just waited—knowing that the movement towards her had to come from him.

And, *dear God,* he wanted to.

He wasn't aware of closing the distance between them, only of knowing that he had. His mouth fastened on hers and he felt the tremble that ran through her body. That first kiss was questioning, almost as though he were testing himself to see whether he could resist her.

But one touch and he was lost. He heard the small guttural sound in the base of his throat and his whole body surged with power. It was primeval. Conquering.

His woman. *His.*

It was like a shot of pure heroin. He wanted more. He wanted her closer.

Years of rigid control, of complete numbness, were gone in a moment. He wanted her more than he'd wanted anything in his entire life. It was all the more urgent because he knew that he couldn't slide his hand under the fine spaghetti straps of her dress. He couldn't lower his head to take her nipple in his mouth…

Dear God… He'd not prayed to anything since the fire, but he was praying now. He wasn't sure what for. Whether it was strength to resist or strength to grasp what she was offering. He simply didn't know.

But he knew, with absolute certainty, she'd no intention of stopping him from doing anything he wanted. Isabella had walked into this room with the express purpose of offering herself as a gift.

It didn't matter that the doors to the secluded swimming pool were open and that a stray reveller might conceivably come that way. It didn't matter that there was the distant sound of conversation and laughter…

In fact, that only made this feel more raw. More essential.

Her hands moved to cradle his face, her fingers splayed out against the scarring on his face. 'Please don't say you shouldn't be doing this.' She breathed the words against his lips. And then she kissed him.

CHAPTER TEN

ISABELLA could feel Domenic's indecision. Then she felt the tremor that ran through his body and she deepened her kiss. It was a moment before his arms tightened convulsively round her.

His tongue wound round hers, teasing and coaxing at the same time. He couldn't leave her tomorrow. She wouldn't let him.

She wanted him to be a part of her life. She needed him to talk to her, to make the huge changes being imposed on her life seem unimportant and petty beside what she was feeling for him.

She wanted him. Wanted this.

It was like a sudden surge of power to know that she wanted him in her life more than she wanted anything else. If he wanted her to leave Niroli she could do it…for him. And she'd do it without any sense of regret…because she'd know that what she was walking towards was better, more exciting, than what she was leaving behind.

But she could only do that if he wanted her, too.

Her hands snaked up to bury themselves in his thick brown hair. Holding him close. Then closer still.

She knew the minute he took a mental step back from her.

'You're being searched for.' His voice was strained, his breath coming unevenly.

Then she heard someone in the distance calling her name. She raised a shaking hand up to her bruised lips.

The voice called again. 'Your Highness? Princess Isabella?'

'That's Angelo. He's Tomasso's deputy,' she whispered, her eyes not leaving Domenic's face. 'They consider this a high-risk situation and Tomasso mobilised the entire team.'

'You probably shouldn't have come.' His hand brushed her cheek, inexpressibly tender.

'Princess Isabella?'

There was going to be no escape—and they both knew it.

Domenic's smile twisted and his eyes glinted down at her. 'You have more in common with Luca than they thought.'

She found her mouth curved into an answering smile, even though she wished Angelo a million miles away. 'If I were like Luca I wouldn't have been found. He has a gift for disappearing.' Then she turned her head and called out. 'I'm here.'

Her bodyguard came into view and stood in sight of the open doors. He looked flushed and a deep frown cracked across his forehead.

'I'm sorry to have worried you,' Isabella said quickly, walking towards him. 'I should have told you where I was going.'

She looked behind her to where Domenic was still standing. His evening jacket was open, his dress shirt open at the neck, his scars clearly visible…and he was the sexiest man she'd ever seen.

He was the only man she'd ever want. Could ever want. Because she loved him. *Loved him.*

Somehow she'd fallen in love with Domenic Vincini. And

her happiness depended on his loving her back. Her grand gesture was no longer about being given the opportunity to explore a mutual attraction. It was about spending a lifetime together. Sharing a future.

And it probably always had been. Nothing was ever going to matter as much as the next few minutes.

Isabella swallowed painfully, acutely conscious of Angelo standing within hearing distance. His face might be turned away and his expression impassive, but that didn't mean he wasn't listening.

She moistened her lips and tried to steady her breathing. 'Come out to the party,' she said huskily. 'I want you with me.'

'I'm better here.'

Domenic was distancing himself again as surely as if he'd turned and walked away. He was looking at her as he might a pleasant memory and she wanted to scream at him, make him understand it didn't have to be like this.

Behind her she could hear Angelo reporting that he'd found her. 'Would it really matter if they took your photograph?' she said, softly.

His hand reached out to hold hers and he moved his thumb across her palm. 'I would hate it.'

'Dom—'

'You go.'

Domenic let go of her hand and Isabella wasn't left with much alternative but to do as he said. She smiled for Angelo's benefit, but inside the cold knot of fear she'd arrived with had returned.

She didn't know how to fight Domenic's resistance. Instinct told her she was going to have to break it down piece by piece.

Isabella stepped outside and walked past the oversized lanterns by the edge of the pool. She didn't look back but she was aware that Domenic watched her go. All the way. And she had no idea whether he would follow her.

Angelo fell into step beside her, saying nothing.

She glanced up. 'I'm sorry.'

'We were worried.' It was as close to a rebuke as he would dare.

'I know.' Isabella lifted the front of her skirts to negotiate the steps that twisted down to the large white marquee. Small white lights had been looped across the vast tented ceiling and beyond it she could see the sea, a warm rosy moon reflected in the water. It was so beautiful her heart ached.

Everywhere there seemed to be people. And noise. The moment she appeared the general hum rose a notch and Angelo remained solidly by her side, ready to protect her if the need arose.

She refused to look back towards the villa. She'd needed him to care about her enough to ignore the hurtful comments and come with her. *She needed him to love her.*

'Did you find him?' Silvana asked, coming to stand beside her. 'I wish he'd—' She broke off as her attention was caught by Domenic appearing at the top of the steps.

Isabella followed the line of her vision and her heart stopped beating.

Both women watched as Alberto insistently called him across to join the group of men he was talking with. Domenic's eyes met hers and a frisson of awareness tingled across the space between them.

'I don't know what you said but I'm glad it worked,'

Silvana said quietly. 'Sometimes I think we should have been harder on him when he first came out of hospital. Made him face people and the crass comments.'

The tiny brunette looked up as the noise of a helicopter drowned out the sound of the orchestra. 'I think that's someone trying to get pictures of the party. That's the second time it's been over in as many minutes.'

'Your Highness?' Tomasso moved swiftly alongside her. 'Perhaps you might like to move out of range?'

Isabella obediently turned towards the lighted marquee. A huge buffet table groaned under goat's cheese, Arab inspired flat breads, roasted peppers shining with olive oil, salami and rice timbales. Marzipan had been carefully fashioned into the shape of strawberries, figs and prickly pears.

'Is it after you?' Domenic asked, coming across the marquee towards her. His eyes looked back to where the helicopter was still circling overhead.

'Probably.' Her chest felt tight and her voice sounded a little breathless. 'If I keep out of sight maybe it'll go away.'

The eyes that met hers were smoky. What she wanted to do was touch him, dance with him, but already she was aware of eyes turning to look at them.

And he'd told her he wasn't ready for that.

Domenic's hand moved to hold his neck, apparently conscious of their stares.

The helicopter circled overhead and the sound of the blades drowned out the orchestra. 'I think I should go. My being here is beginning to cause a problem. W-will we get a chance to talk back at the palazzo, do you think?'

She could see his throat work painfully. 'Isabella...' He broke off and tried again. 'What would we say?'

'We could—'

'What?' His voice rose and she saw the conscious effort he made to lower it. 'Arrange to meet in Rome? Or do you think I could visit you on Niroli?'

Tears stung the back of her eyes.

'This isn't going to happen.'

Isabella bit down hard on her bottom lip. *Finally,* she'd fallen in love. She'd met the man she wanted to spend the rest of her life with…and she was fairly sure he was in love with her.

But that wasn't enough. Domenic wouldn't let her into his life. And tomorrow he'd be gone.

The helicopter turned and made another circuit. Everyone had stopped what they were doing to look. Isabella blinked hard, fighting back the tears.

'Are you wanting to leave, Your Highness?' Tomasso asked, coming to stand beside her.

This scenario wasn't new. Many, many times she'd been covertly led away from intrusive reporters but she'd never found leaving anywhere so difficult. 'I think so.'

'Very good, Your Highness.' She was aware of his quietly voiced instructions to a colleague. Her car would be brought up to the villa. In minutes she'd be speeding away…

'Silvana is staying on Mont Avellana until you leave.'

Domenic's eyes seemed to hold hers and her throat felt dry and ripped raw.

'And I'll have my lawyers contact yours about moving forward with the resort.'

She nodded, knowing her voice wouldn't work. *This couldn't be it. It couldn't.*

'Your Highness…' Tomasso stepped in closer. 'Your car is ready.'

It was only a full decade of royal experience that meant she smiled as she walked away.

Domenic turned his car into the long sweeping driveway of the palazzo, pleased to see every window was in darkness. He'd half expected Isabella would be waiting for him.

At least, he *should* have been pleased to see it was in darkness. It was what he'd told her he wanted.

And there was nothing to be gained from a long and painful goodbye. Nothing that needed explaining.

The tyres made a satisfying crunch on the gravel as he pulled the Ferrari to a stop outside the central main doors. Normally he would take it round the back to the garages, but tonight he felt too weary.

Or too heartsore?

He'd allow himself a short sleep and then he'd leave for Rome. He might even be gone before Isabella was awake. It would be best if he was gone before she was awake. He glanced up at the window of her bedroom. Heavy lace panels billowed out of the open doors leading onto her balcony.

Domenic gripped his car keys so tightly they left marks on the palm of his hand. He pushed open the heavy doorway and walked into the darkened entrance hall. A sudden flash of white had him looking upwards.

And he knew what he would see. *Who*.

Isabella stood up from the stair she'd been sitting on. She'd changed into a simple white T-shirt and skirt and no longer seemed like a woman who graced red carpets across Europe. She looked approachable, fresh and beautiful.

His.

Against the ornate backdrop of the dramatic central staircase she even looked a little out of place. Her hair hung loose and softly about her face. Her lips trembled.

He put a foot on the bottom stair. 'I thought you'd be asleep.'

'No.'

Happiness came crashing in around him and scared him with its power.

'Did Alberto enjoy the rest of his party?'

'He's still going.' Domenic climbed the rest of the stairs until he stood level. 'His particular friends won't leave until after breakfast.'

'Did the helicopter return?'

'No.' He pulled his hand across his neck. 'No, it didn't.'

She nodded. 'It followed my car back here, and then left. I-I hoped it wouldn't.' Her eyes hovered on his mouth and he felt as if a hand had reached inside him and squeezed his heart hard.

'He was glad you came.'

'I came for you.' Her words hit him with the force of a sledgehammer. Her brown eyes met his.

'Isa—'

She stopped him. 'Don't! Please don't tell me it's not a good idea.'

Domenic reached out a hand and flicked the nearby switch. Light flooded the upper landing and picked out the tiny crystal flecks in the stone staircase. 'Even though it isn't? This isn't some kind of a game. Take a good look at me, Isabella.'

Her eyes remained steadily on his face. 'I love you.'

'No! Really look at me.' His hand pulled open the neck of his white shirt. 'Look at it.'

'You're scarred,' she said quietly.

His let the fabric go and violently dragged the same hand through his hair.

'It doesn't make any difference. I still love you.'

Domenic pulled in a breath. 'You think you do, but you're living in some kind of fantasy.'

'I think you should have more faith in me,' she said on a spurt of anger. 'I know what I'm feeling.'

'This is madness!'

'Why?'

'You want me to list the reasons? Really? Do you really want me to do that?'

Isabella moved towards him for the first time, resting her hand on his arm. Even through his dinner jacket her hand seemed to touch his skin. 'There are solutions to all of them.'

He shook his head. 'Not this one,' he said, with a gesture at his face.

'I love you. I want to be with you.'

'You say that now, but sooner or later you'd leave me. You'd get tired of people whispering every time they saw us together. Tired of having to look at a face like this. I've had enough pain in my life. No more. I don't want any more.'

Isabella's chin came up and she met his eyes. 'So you've decided you have to leave me first? Is that it?'

'It's not like that—'

'It's exactly like that! *Damn it!* Aren't you stronger than that? Braver?' She drew a shaky breath and her hand reached up and touched the side of his face. Her palms were cool against his cheek. She stepped closer and stood on tiptoe. 'Who managed to convince you no one could love you?'

'I—'

'They lied, Domenic. I love you. *You.*'

Her hair brushed the underside of his jaw as she let her hands run down across his shoulders and slip inside his jacket. Slowly, deliberately, she took the weight of his dinner jacket and pushed it off his shoulders.

He felt a shudder pass through his body. It felt as if every negative comment he'd overheard was warring with what she was telling him. Was it a weakness in him to want to believe?

The bow tie he wore but hadn't tied followed his jacket. Then she reached up and kissed him. His lips seemed to have taken on a will of their own. 'Let it happen,' she murmured against his mouth. 'Just let it happen.'

He wanted to, with every fibre of his being.

His hands moved of their own volition, pulling her in hard against his arousal. 'This is madness.'

'Be mad.'

Domenic ran a finger along her collarbone and pressed a kiss against the pulse at the base of her neck. Her head fell back and he ran the tip of his tongue up the length of her neck.

Then he found her mouth. Warm and sensual. He'd kissed her before. Each time had been memorable but *this* time he knew it was the prelude to something more. This time it seemed to reach into his soul and draw it into her.

He heard the moan rip from her throat and he felt the answering surge of power within him. His hands buried themselves in the sweet smelling softness of her hair, while hers fisted in the fabric of his shirt.

Another moment more and he'd make love to her on the landing. Laughter bubbled up inside him and he pulled away. 'We—'

She placed a hand over his mouth. 'Don't speak.' Her eyes

were gleaming. She took hold of his hand and led him towards her bedroom.

This *was* madness. He knew it as she shut the door behind them…but forgot it when her hands reached up to unbutton his shirt. Her fingers stroked down his ribs, pushing the cotton aside.

Her eyes locked with his as she slowly moved up to caress the bare skin of his shoulders. One side smooth, the other puckered and twisted. He tensed and she stood up on tiptoe to kiss his mouth while her fingers smoothed out the tension.

'Trust me.'

And, unbelievably, he did. Slowly she eased the cotton over his shoulders and let her fingers trail down his arms.

'I've never seduced a man before.' Her fingers moved to link with his. 'I'm not sure I know how to do it.'

He stared into her eyes for a moment and then moved. Her lips were warm and trembling as he kissed her. He could feel her nervousness and it made him love her more. He hadn't believed that was possible either.

'Am I doing it right?' she whispered against his lips.

'I'd say you had it about perfect.' He inhaled deeply and moved her hands to rest on his chest. Her fingers splayed out and then she let them slide down the narrow line of hair that ran down the hard plane of his stomach.

The muscles of his stomach quivered and he kissed her again. His own hands ran down her arms and reached for the bottom of her T-shirt. For a moment he hesitated. Her eyes met his and then she stepped back and raised her arms.

Domenic pulled her top over her head and his eyes fell on the deep pink of her nipples pushing up hard against the white transparent material of her bra. He let the T-shirt fall onto the floor and moved his thumb to brush against the tip.

Her white teeth bit down on her bottom lip and she shivered. 'Are you sure you want this?' *Want me,* he added silently.

Her answer was to reach in front and unclip the central fastening of her bra. It fell open and his hands smoothed it away.

Dark nipples against pale skin. Round, full breasts. He watched amazed as she moved closer so they brushed against the darker skin of his chest. She looped one finger into the top of his trousers and pulled him towards her. 'Take me to bed.'

CHAPTER ELEVEN

ISABELLA woke quite suddenly and knew she was alone in the bed. She rolled over, taking the sheet with her. Domenic was standing by the doors to the balcony, lost in thought, and he'd been up long enough to have pulled on his trousers.

All her euphoric certainty of the night before evaporated. 'Have you been awake long?'

'I haven't slept,' he said without turning round.

Isabella sat up and pushed her hair back from her face. They'd made love—but it changed *nothing*. 'Domenic?'

'Go back to sleep.'

She flicked her long legs out of bed and padded across to him, wrapping the sheet around her as she went. Then she laid her cheek against his bare back and put her arms around him. 'You're still going, aren't you?'

He nodded and she felt a huge sob well up inside her. 'Why?'

He turned and pulled her up close against him, rubbing his face against the top of her head. 'I think you know that—'

'I could go with you.'

'Not without bringing the world's press with you. A-and I can't live like that.' Domenic dragged a breath in and let his hands rest on her shoulders. His fingers were warm on her skin and then he let the palms of his hands slide down her arms. 'We need to talk.'

They had to be the most frightening words in the universe. They didn't need to talk. They needed to kiss and to hold each other…

Isabella let him lead her back towards the bed. Why was he doing this? He loved her. She knew it. He might not have said the words, but she'd seen it in his eyes, felt it.

His hand stretched out to cup her face and he drew her in for a kiss. It was soft, healing…but far too brief. Domenic pulled back and looked into her eyes. 'Should we have taken precautions?'

Her mind took a moment to shift into gear. Precautions? She didn't know what he was talking about. And then she understood. A baby. He was asking whether they might have made a baby together.

And she felt numb. 'No. At least, yes.' Isabella pulled a hand through her tangled curls. 'I suppose it's possible…but, no. I don't think so. It's not the right time of the month.'

And the dreadful truth was she wouldn't care if she was pregnant with his baby. Particularly if it kept him with her. Was that wicked? To wish she had a way of tying him to her?

'I didn't think. I'm sorry…'

Isabella looked down to where he'd laid his hand over hers. Long, beautiful fingers stretched out on hers. He moved his thumb in an agonising sweep across the back of her hand.

'We didn't plan on last night.' She swallowed, trying to force down the hard ball of unshed tears that were wedged at the base of her throat. 'It just happened. We were—'

His thumb moved again. 'I should have thought about it, but Jolanda was the only woman I've ever made love to.'

Until last night. Isabella looked up. She hadn't expected that and yet, the more she thought about it, the more she thought she should have done.

'I've never had a lifestyle where I've needed to carry condoms in my top pocket. I'm sorry.'

'You wouldn't be here if I thought you were.' Her voice cracked. 'W-was it difficult? To be with me, I mean?'

'No. No.' His hand moved swiftly to hold her face, his thumb brushed the sensitive skin beneath her right eye. 'But I should have thought about the possibility of making you pregnant.'

'You won't have.'

The thought of having his baby made her melt. Why couldn't he smile at her and tell her it wouldn't matter? Why couldn't he say he loved her and wanted to build a family with her?

'I can't believe I've been so thoughtless.' Domenic turned away and walked restlessly back towards the French doors.

She sat further back on the bed and covered her body with the sheet and watched him. This felt a little like dying inside. It was crueller, harder, because she'd allowed herself to hope.

'When are you going?' Her voice was hollow, completely toneless.

'Today. Now.'

Pain licked through her.

'I think it's best.'

'For who exactly?' The question burst like the cork from shaken lemonade. 'It's not best for me.'

His eyes settled on her face. Then he sat down on the edge of the bed. 'Do you want children?'

'Yes.' Isabella gasped in air. 'One day. Not straight away necessarily but, yes, I'd like children.' His children. She desperately wanted to have his children.

'I don't.' He pulled a shaky hand through his hair. Then his eyes searched hers for understanding. 'I don't ever want children. I couldn't…do that. Not again.'

The words seemed to back up in his throat so he couldn't get them out. Isabella sat forward. 'I know it would be difficult—'

'No, you don't know!' There was shocked silence as his voice echoed around the room. 'I'm sorry. But you don't know. You couldn't.' His hand balled into a fist as he punched his frustration. 'Every morning I wake up and I feel sick inside because I couldn't save them. It's a living nightmare. And it keeps going on and on. Day after day.

'I keep breathing in and out, pushing myself to keep on going, because I don't have an alternative. But don't think I haven't thought about it. I've thought about it.

'In the early days I even tried drinking myself into oblivion. It feels like I'm being dissected piece by piece. I'm not…*able*…' he pulled the word out with immense difficulty '…to do everything again.'

'It would be different—'

'You belong with someone who isn't…*tortured* by memories they can't control.'

'I could help and we could take things slowly. We—'

'I don't want to love you.'

Isabella felt the effect of that like a gunshot. He didn't want to love her. Didn't *want* to. She looked up, her eyes stinging.

'You're right. This is about being brave enough. *Strong* enough. And I'm not strong enough to live with the risk of losing you.' His teeth clenched together and a pulse flickered in his cheek. 'I can't have children with you and watch them grow and think about the one I couldn't save. I can't do that.'

'It wasn't your fault.'

His eyes were shining and then one tear welled up and rolled slowly down his cheek in one glistening trail. Isabella felt a searing pain as she watched, powerless to do anything to help him. *Powerless to change it.*

'I don't want to love anyone or anything so much that I can't face losing them. I…' His voice cracked and he raised a hand to cover his eyes.

Isabella moved on pure instinct. She pushed the sheet aside and went to him. Her arms went round him and she cradled him into her, her cheek resting against the scarred tissue of his shoulder.

She knew something about pain. The loss of her parents had been sudden, dramatic and disorientating. She knew what it felt like to wake and be flooded by fresh grief.

Her arms tightened about him. Then she pressed small kisses against his chest. She heard him groan and his hands tangle in her long curls. He tipped her face up and he kissed her.

Isabella made an incoherent little sound as his fingers skimmed her bare back, gossamer light. She wasn't sure what she was thinking, or even if she was thinking at all.

Isabella arched against him and his mouth firmed over hers. Her lips parted involuntarily at the pressure of his mouth and his tongue was ruthless.

This felt desperate.

He might not want to love her but he couldn't resist her. If she just had a little more time. Time to convince him it was already too late to decide he didn't love her. Didn't *want* to.

He pulled back like a man drowning and she'd never seen him look so bleak. Often, in repose, his face fell into lines of sadness, but this was something more.

Her hand went out. 'Domenic—'

'If I kiss you any more I'll make love to you again,' he said, catching her hand and holding it.

'Would that be so bad?'

'And you could have my baby in nine months. This is already complicated enough. I need to go.'

Isabella felt an unbelievable sense of desperation. Her fingers convulsively closed round his. 'Not yet. Don't leave me yet.'

She could feel the tension in his hand. The war that was going on between what he wanted and what he felt was right. 'You could just hold me—'

Domenic shook his head. 'If I did that I'd kiss you and when I kiss you I want to make love to you.'

'I want you to. I won't get pregnant.' Tears ran silently down her face. 'I won't.'

'You can't know that. Not for sure.' The muscle pulsed in the side of his jaw. 'Isabella, I can't be what you want. And I need to go while I still can.'

Inside she felt raw, as though she'd been flayed until she had no skin left. 'Spend the day with me.' Her voice was as broken as she felt. 'Just one more day.'

The grip of his fingers on her shoulders tightened and words tumbled out of her mouth. 'Don't leave me like this. We could spend it here in the grounds of the palazzo. No one would see us. One more day before we let the world back in.'

The muscle pulsed in the side of his cheek. 'I need to go.' He stood up and let his hand slide from hers.

Isabella watched as he picked up his shirt and walked out of the room. For a moment she felt nothing—and then the pain splintered through her like shrapnel.

* * *

Domenic pulled his hand over his face and walked over to the water cooler. Isabella's letter sat on the desk unopened.

Missing her felt like a physical ache. It was a constant, gnawing pain. He took the cup back to his desk and sat looking at the cardboard backed envelope.

He knew what was in it. Photographs of the morning they'd spent at Poseidon's Grotto. Could he bear to see them? To remember?

Could he bear not to?

His fingers ripped open the top and a sheaf of glossy prints fell out onto his black desk. Beautiful, *beautiful* pictures.

There were the steps down the limestone cliff. The view out across to the Spanish watchtower. A seabird soaring high in a bright blue sky. He really ought to pass them on to someone who could contact her about using these images. Certainly if they decided to build the grotto up into a tourist attraction…

Isabella had a real talent. He'd been there and had seen the views she'd taken, but he hadn't seen it with her eye for detail. He hadn't noticed the shadow cast by the juniper plant. The changes of colour across the limestone cliff.

He wished he could tell her.

Then he came to the last in the sheaf and he stopped breathing. A photograph he hadn't known she'd taken. One he'd forbidden. His hand splayed out on top of it because it was almost too painful to look at.

Isabella had taken a picture of him. He was concentrating on unpacking their picnic, unconscious of the camera. And she'd spared him nothing. He could see the twisted skin of his neck, the slashes across his face. And yet it was a picture taken with love.

Every image she captured seemed to ring with truth and passion. It started when she made a decision to take a picture.

Understanding hit him like a sledgehammer. *He was such an idiot.*

He'd thrown away the chance of unconditional acceptance because he was too afraid of rejection. She'd seen him, *really seen him,* and she still loved him.

Loved him enough to push aside centuries of resentment between their islands. Loved him enough to face the criticism of her family. Loved him despite the superficial scars on his face and the deeper trauma that had forged his personality.

She had told him. 'I love *you*'. And on some level he'd heard the stress she'd placed on the word 'you'.

Domenic turned the photograph over and saw the three words she'd written on the back. 'I miss you.'

Isabella stepped out of the car into the flash of cameras. For the past ten days the attention on her had been constant. Exhausting. News that she'd clinched the biggest deal in Niroli's history had spread like ink through water.

Her success had even gone some way to pacifying her grandfather. He'd been inclined to think her contact with the Vincini family had been a necessary evil.

She stopped while a young girl nervously presented her with a bouquet of yellow roses and forced herself to smile. It was important to her that her grief remained private. But she longed to move away from Niroli and find some anonymity.

It was funny that, having achieved what she'd thought would enable her to stay on the island, she'd no desire to do so. The truth was she wanted to be where Domenic was.

But more than that. She wanted a quieter life. Her time on Mont Avellana had taught her so many things about herself. Now her 'duty' to Niroli didn't require her to travel so many air miles she'd prefer not to.

She wanted to pursue her photography and take it to a new level of creativity. She wanted to allow more time and space for friends.

And it was possible. For the first time in a decade, it *was* a viable choice. All this was Nico's responsibility now. He could promote Niroli's film industry. He could shake the hands of the producer, director, director's wife…

Isabella moved on down the line while the cameras flashed all around her. She responded appropriately to Signore Lanza's comments about not forgetting his cinematic roots now he'd moved from smaller art-house movies to big-budget films. And she stopped to allow the gathered photographers to capture her image alongside the 'A'-list actor who played the central character.

As she was about to move inside the carefully restored art deco building she looked back at the lines of people banked up either side of a sweeping red carpet. She lifted her hand to give a final wave…

And then she saw him. Domenic. Darkly handsome in black dinner jacket, his shirt open at the neck, his hands thrust deep in his dinner jacket.

His eyes looking directly at her.

For a few seconds nothing made sense. There was a part of her that wondered whether she might have conjured him up because she wanted him with her so badly.

Around her the crowds disappeared into a blur of indistinct colour. He was here. *Domenic was here on Niroli.*

'Your Highness.' Tomasso was urging her inside but she felt her feet moving the other way.

'Excuse me,' she murmured, walking back down the broad steps. 'I'm so sorry, excuse me.'

Domenic was held back from her by a low-slung red rope. Police and security guards lined the sides and banks of reporters were clustered to her left. In some strange way she was aware of it all but she kept looking at Domenic's face, trying to read the expression in his eyes.

Why was he here? Had he changed his mind? Was he here for her?

She stopped a few feet away from him.

His smile twisted into a kind of wry apology. His eyes were holding hers. 'I thought it was time I was…braver.'

'Past time.'

'Am I too late?'

Isabella shook her head as a tremulous happiness quivered inside her. 'No.'

Lights flashed all around them but Domenic was unflinching. With a glance across at one of the security guards he climbed over the low roping. 'I got your message. I miss you, too.'

There was a sudden cheer and excited whispering as people in the crowd caught a glimpse of what was happening. Isabella felt a bubble of laughter. 'What are you doing?'

'Doing what I should have done at my father's party.' He stopped in front of her. 'I love you.'

Isabella couldn't breathe. She couldn't quite believe he was here…or what he was saying. Most of all she couldn't believe what he was saying.

'I love you more than I fear this.'

She gave a sudden laugh and reached for his hand. The

crowd went berserk. Reporters pressed forward and Tomasso gestured security guards to create a ring around them. 'Your Highness,' he prompted. 'We need to move inside.'

Isabella kept her eyes on Domenic. 'You know they'll be able to lip-read everything you've said.'

He smiled and her stomach flipped over.

'Your Highness. Please.' Tomasso became more insistent.

Laughter spilled over. She'd never felt happiness like this.

'Princess Isabella!'

She turned to look at Tomasso and then back at Domenic. Her fingers felt small and safe within his hand. 'Shall we go inside?'

His eyes flicked down to their joined hands. 'I'll go anywhere you go.'

It was a promise. All the way back up the red carpet she didn't take her eyes off him. It was too incredible he was here with her. There were shouts and cheers. People calling her name and asking her his.

Tomasso cleared the path before them and led them into a small office immediately off the grand entrance. As the door shut behind them Isabella suddenly felt shy. She looked down at his shiny black shoes.

'I wasn't sure you'd forgive me for being such a fool,' he said quietly.

Isabella reached up and touched the scars on his face. 'I thought this was your worst nightmare?'

'So did I. But then I discovered losing you was a worse one.'

She let her thumb brush against his bottom lip. He took it into his mouth and nibbled against it. Isabella gave a sob of sheer happiness and his arms closed about her. 'I love you. I love—'

And then he was kissing her as though she was the most

precious thing in his world. 'Marry me?' he said, pulling away. 'Be my wife? Have children with me?'

'Children?' Her hand splayed out on his chest.

His eyes were warm and his touch gentle as they brushed away the single tear that tipped over onto her cheek. 'Sometime. When you're ready.'

'I'm ready,' she said on a husky whisper. 'But you—'

'Nearly lost the best thing that had ever happened to me. Silvana said that.'

'She did?'

He nodded. 'At my father's party.'

There was a sharp knock at the door. 'Princess Isabella?'

She brushed her fingers beneath her eyes. 'They want to start the movie. Is my make-up all right?'

'You're beautiful,' he said, hanging back.

Her hand came back to rest in his. 'Come with me.'

'I don't have a seat.'

Isabella felt her laughter bubble over. 'They'll find you one. It's the only advantage I know in being in a relationship with a princess.'

'There are others.' His hands spanned her waist and turned her. 'Are you going to marry me?'

'Oh, yes.'

His eyes moved over her face. 'Even if you have to leave Niroli?'

'Even then.' She reached up to kiss him. 'Yes, please.'

EPILOGUE

AWAY from the streetlights the night sky was a million dots of light. Isabella felt small, insignificant…and perfectly happy.

She turned her head as she heard Domenic walk up behind her. He pulled her against his body and she felt his arousal hard against the small of her back. Then he bent his head and placed a kiss at the base of her neck.

'Tired?'

Isabella turned within his arms. 'Not really.' Her smile was deliberately teasing and she watched the laughter glint deep in his brown eyes. She reached up a hand and smoothed back the hair from his forehead, then let it run down the side of his face.

He caught it, and held it against his chest. 'You have to know…'

Beneath her fingers she could feel the steady beat of his heart.

'I want you to know that I've never done anything in my entire life I've been more sure of.'

Isabella understood what he was trying to tell her. There had been moments during their simple church wedding and at the family gathering at Silvana's villa when she'd wondered how much of his mind was on Jolanda. And little Felice.

'Jolanda helped make you the man I love.'

His fingers tightened around hers. 'I was happy then. I'm happy now.' His eyes moved to her lips. 'And I didn't think I'd ever be happy again.'

She'd thought she didn't feel any kind of fear at being the second wife of a man who had so deeply loved his first one, but in that moment she realised Domenic had been wiser than her. Seen more.

He placed a kiss against her lips and pulled back to murmur, 'I love you. With everything that I am and everything that I have.'

And when he kissed her again she felt a new warmth spread through her body. A feeling of total acceptance. Of simply being right for him because of who she was.

His hands moved against the fine silk of her wedding dress and spread out across her buttocks, pulling her in closer still. She threw back her head and laughed, giving him access to the long column of her throat.

She breathed his name as he kissed down her neck and sought out the pulse at its base. 'I love you, too.' Her eyes sought his. 'With everything that I am and everything that I have.'

He smiled at the echo of his words and then he found her hand to lead her back towards the villa. 'Are you sorry we chose to come here?'

'To our own private island?' Isabella moved in closer and placed an arm about his waist, loving the feeling of his body so close to hers and the warm sand beneath her bare feet. 'Whatever we decide to do and develop, we must always keep Teulada for ourselves. Our own little bit of paradise.'

His fingers moved in her curls. He led her up onto the wide raised decking and pulled her down onto a pile of cushions. Far out across the dark sea were the lights of Niroli, clearly visible now they were out beyond the jutting limestone cliffs of Mont Avellana.

It looked beautiful. Romantic. But Isabella knew there was nowhere else she'd rather be.

Domenic kept his eyes on her profile. 'I wish your family could have been there for you today.'

'Yours were.'

'But your brother. Sister.'

Isabella shook her head. 'Marco's Emily is pregnant and doesn't want to fly. And I don't want to make Rosa's life difficult. I know she loves me. That's enough.'

'And King Giorgio? Niroli?'

She turned to look at him. 'I'd give up more than that to be with you.'

'I wish you hadn't had to.'

Isabella pulled herself up on the cushions and moved into his arms. 'It won't be for ever. When Nico arrives everything will change again. Once Grandfather is happy that Niroli will be in safe hands after he's gone he'll lose much of his anger.'

Domenic pressed a kiss on the top of her head. She looked up at him and smiled. Her eyes took on a teasing glint. 'Now stop talking…and kiss me.'

She watched his eyes darken and her stomach tightened in anticipation as he bent his head to do just that.

* * * * *

As Princess Isabella chooses to leave her home of Niroli and start a new life with the man she loves, across the waters, another heart-wrenching decision is being made…

SLAMMING his fist hard into the sandstone wall brought no respite to his mind but gave his body the much needed release it craved. Blood dripped steadily onto the cold marble tiles as he walked to the balcony that overlooked his kingdom. Below him he could see the hustle and bustle of the market and, in front, a thousand rooftops—the homes of his people. His people! He smacked his hand down again, the cool of the tiles on his palm drawing the fierce heat of his rage.

He turned away and moved to the simple wooden bench where he had sat, so many times in the past, and gazed out over the horizon of his kingdom. A view that had calmed him by showing him the people he had been chosen to protect. A view that no longer belonged to him, a role that was no longer his, a role that had never really been his… He had to leave his people. And when he remembered that, the heat of his anger rose again.

* * * * *

*Why must this man leave the people he loves
and what impact will this have on the ruling
Fierezza family of Niroli?
Don't miss EXPECTING HIS ROYAL BABY
to find out more.*

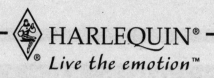

HARLEQUIN®

Live the emotion™

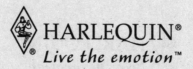

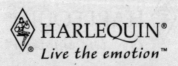

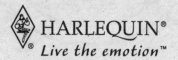

Harlequin® Historical
Historical Romantic Adventure!

Imagine a time of chivalrous knights and unconventional ladies, roguish rakes and impetuous heiresses, rugged cowboys and spirited frontierswomen— these rich and vivid tales will capture your imagination!

Harlequin Historical . . . they're too good to miss!